C. L. DONLEY

Rich Little Poor Girl

This book was professionally typeset on Reedsy.
Find out more at reedsy.com

Contents

Prologue: Ten Years Ago

Solomon Dvorak doesn't see— only hears— the young cafeteria worker walk out of the room as he looks down from the 45th floor of his corner office, down at the empire that his father built, that he's managed to continue in the same tradition.

His blue eyes are vivid yet uninviting, his marble stone features sterile and wrinkled. He feels a tremor in his hand, in his own brain, and wonders just how much time he has left.

But he only wonders, refusing to ever have it confirmed. His father had allowed a doctor to declare a deadline over his existence, and he'd naively rushed to meet it. Solomon would not be following in his footsteps.

He supposed it was too much to ask for God to spare his family another medical clusterfuck. So he didn't ask.

Any minute now, his son was probably going to come storming in here, pigeon-toed and angry. Because Solomon had done yet another thing for his own good.

It vexed him to no end that Ben walked around the building without his crutches, waddling around like some fucking aquatic bird. An unintended consequence of being born a Dvorak. Who would dare tell him that they all pitied him and thought he was a freak? Everyone kept calling him "brave," and Solomon was forced to hide his disdain for his son's private rebellion.

"Mr. Dvorak, your son is here to see you," his intercom warbles.

Solomon Dvorak feigned ignorance.

"I have two sons, Margaret, which one are you referring to?"

Sure enough, before Margaret could answer, Ben roared through the double doors in his usual sharp dress, his scissor walk over-pronounced, his espresso brown eyes blazing but not particularly threatening.

Not like his older brother Grant, a young version of his own father, intimidating and sure, like a lion. Ben was more like a very stern puppy. Good for nothing but attracting women and getting people to buy things they wouldn't otherwise.

Not entirely useless. Solomon's last resort, you could say.

Today, the puppy was baring his teeth.

"What the hell's going on? Was Cynthia fired?"

"Back from lunch already, Mr. Dvorak?" Solomon said to his son, "I think the quants downstairs are still awaiting your contribution."

"Look, whatever you have against me, take it out on me," said Ben, breathless with anger. "If you ever want this company to outlive you, you'll stay out of my personal life!"

"You insult me, Benjamin. What brought Miss Gordon to my office was a professional matter."

"Since when does a cafeteria worker need to speak to the CEO of the Dvorak Group?"

"It was a very serious professional matter."

"The mashed potato serving sizes are too big dad? Save it," Ben wrinkled his brow in disbelief. "Why can't you admit that you're trying to run my life, the way you've tried to run everyone else's?"

"I know you well enough to know that trying to run your life is beyond my powers."

Benjamin's eyes blazed. His square jaw ticked. "What did you say to her?"

"I told her that she is terminated effective immediately and that for the sake of my son, we won't be pressing charges."

Ben just stood there stunned. "What the hell is wrong with you?" he marveled.

"I have it on good authority that Miss Gordon had extensive plans to sabotage the company. Plans that involved you."

"'On the good authority' of whom, one of your goons? I don't want to hear anymore. You'll say anything to get what you want."

"Not true," Sol answered stoically. "You think I don't want you to be happy, son? Everything I do, I do it for the family, Benjamin."

"Is that why Mom left? And Grant's a fucking basket case? Because of all your magnanimous sacrifices?"

"Your mother didn't 'leave.' Moving your mother's treasure chest of belongings from Scarsdale to a Manhattan apartment hardly deserves the term."

Ben's handsome young face looked etched in a permanent scowl as he launched a second set of gross accusations, half hoping they weren't true. If so, it meant he was surrounded by traitors.

"Was this your call? Or Melanie's?"

His father's familiar manipulative cadence confirmed it was true.

"Melanie was concerned. I looked into the matter for her, that's all."

"There is no 'matter.' Cynthia's a friend. A *good* friend, and one of your best employees. She doesn't deserve this," Ben pleaded.

Good indeed, his father thought with a faint smirk, his long bony fingers pointing into a pyramid as he spoke like a movie villain.

"I applaud your... diplomatic language son. You'll need it in the future. But honestly, you can't be so sloppy about these things," he said, moving from his chair to sitting on the edge of his large polished desk. "I understand your insistence to start at the bottom, and I admire it. It's commendable. But it's not necessary. Not if it leads you to forget who you actually are."

Ben shook his head with a laugh. "This is fucking insane! I'm here, aren't I? I want to be! I'm doing what you wanted, I'm taking over the business! You really think I'm going to let you imprison me like this?" The present company in the room hadn't moved, as if it were another typical board meeting.

"Ben, don't be so dramatic. You imprisoned your own self with your recklessness. You have a fiancée who's concerned. Who, instead of becoming jealous and unruly and calling things off, did the right thing, the prudent thing, and asked for help. You've humiliated her, and you will make it up to her."

"I'm going to make it up to her by calling it off. She doesn't deserve me, and I'm too young to be doing this."

"I would agree with you in this case, but if you're throwing away a good match just to chase a cafeteria worker—"

"I'm going after her, Dad. Whether you want me to or not," Ben smirked with disdain, his perfect white teeth unwittingly lighting the room a moment. "There's nothing you can say to convince me she's guilty of whatever your 'good authority' has cooked up."

"I figured as much," Solomon sighed, feigning deference. "Honestly, I hope you find her. I suspect she'll leave town to avoid investigation, but I'm a romantic at heart too, Benjamin."

"What are you talking about?" Ben glared.

"I'm saying I hope I'm wrong. She's very bright. Smart. Tough. She called me a cunt."

"She what?"

"I can see why she captured your... imagination."

Ben put his tongue in his cheek. "Okay, I'll bite."

"Bite what?"

"Cut the bullshit dad, why would Cynthia leave town?"

"I promised her that I wouldn't tell you the details."

"I see."

"It was part of our... deal. For a petty deceiver, she seems to care a great deal about your opinion of her."

Ben ran a hand through his short dark hair. He licked his naturally pouted lips.

"Fine. It looks like I'm going to have to find out for myself."

"Benjamin, your judgment has been severely clouded by this young lady. I doubt your search will result in the truth. If she is innocent, then let her come to you. That is my advice."

"Screw your advice."

"Did Miss Gordon tell you anything about how she came to work here?"

Benjamin shifted his head a bit and furrowed his thick brows. What was the old man on about now?

"The new cafeteria manager. Poached her from the last place he worked, what of it?"

"Did you know her mother was laid off a year ago by the Delco Plant, a Dvorak subsidiary?"

"No."

"And that her mother was sold a subprime mortgage loan by Penny-Wilde, who sold it to Century Acquisitions, now also a Dvorak company?"

"What the hell does this have to do with anything?"

"It appears your sweet kitchen wench isn't who she said she was. I'll simply leave it at that."

Ben gave his old man a squint before he shook his head as if fending off a spell.

"I can't listen to anymore. I'm going to find Cynthia. And if you try to stop me, I'll quit."

"You'll do more than quit, Benjamin. You'll leave and never return."

"Don't threaten me with a good time, Dad."

"Where will you go? What will do?"

"Stop pretending to be concerned," Ben straightened the cuffs on his dress shirt, accidentally mirroring his father. "Besides, I can figure that out after school."

"Surely you don't expect me to pay for that anymore. Your little private savings would barely cover a semester."

Ben huffed. Of course, his dad knew about his private savings. Still, he was immovable.

"Fine. I'm sure there are plenty of places I can go with an undergrad degree in finance and the last name Dvorak."

"Not if I call in a favor at every other investment bank between here and China," his father threatened.

Ben stood there in a silent stand-off. Instead of going off in a rage, he just laughed.

"All this? To keep me from chasing after some girl? What does she have on you?"

"All this, Benjamin, to keep you from ruining your life and running what I've built into the ground," Sol insisted.

"There's more than one way to do business, Dad. What, you're gonna let Doug run this place?"

"Doug has been with me almost as long as you've been alive."

"And I'm sure he knows where aaall the bodies are buried. If you want to give the family business to a depraved opportunist just to spite me, then you may as well disown me anyway."

"Valerie and Grant will get everything. Based solely on the condition that you get nothing," Sol declared, the desperation only in his words, not his voice.

Ben was further stunned. This time it wasn't amusing.

"Well. It's nice to see how you really feel about being a father. Dad."

"That's your one problem, Benjamin. You still insist on referencing your feelings, as though they could possibly be relevant. You're an investment banker, son. If you want to grow a conscience at the last minute, by all means, chase your conniving bed wench. You'll have a full range of feelings at your disposal then. The only thing you won't have is access to any more of my finances. You'll see how important feelings are then, Benjamin. You'll be very knowledgeable. Knowledgable and poor. It's a wretched state to be in— or so I've heard."

Ben felt pain and anger welling up inside him, but the last thing he would ever do is let his father see that he'd hurt him.

Ben was suddenly finding out that he was too chicken shit to go after the woman he loved, too spineless to be happy. With brute force, he cut the cord to his emotions.

"You're a monster," was all he said.

"Yes, yes. You all keep saying this," Solomon said with a dismissive wave of his hand. "It's a good thing I never had this sentimental problem that you have, or else I may not be able to come to work every day and provide for you ungrateful lot. I'll need your resignation notice by the end of the day, by the way. In case you're truly serious about this little tantrum of yours. You may as well head to your mother's house because your apartment locks will be changed."

"Suck a bag of dicks, Dad."

"Or, you could... do nothing. And I'll assume you're ready to put your grown-up britches on and act like an adult. And in that case, I'll see you bright and early tomorrow."

"The earliest, you bastard," Ben said, steeling his resolve to come up with a plan to escape his father's stranglehold on his life. "You've taken away the one thing that would've kept me in line, Dad. For now, I'm going to play your little game. Until I'm the best at it. And then I'm going to beat *you* at it. This company will be mine. And when it is, my first order of business will be to fire that fat *fuck*," Ben replied, referring to Doug, who was in the room. Ben pointed directly to him without taking his eyes off his father.

His father smiled as Ben turned on his tiptoes, in his familiar bowed and labored gait. It was his first official occasion standing up to the old man. Sol only wished it wasn't over *her*.

"I'm genuinely glad we understand each other better, Mr. Dvorak."

"Go to hell," Ben replied as he walked out of the high double doors.

1

Present Day

"Mr. Dvorak, Evan is here to see you."

"Send him in, Lisa."

Benjamin Dvorak finds himself in the spacious corner office that once belonged to his father, sitting behind the massive cherry wood desk that holds 101 memories. Almost as many as the hospital. Almost.

For the first time in ten years, there's only one Mr. Dvorak at the company again. But for the first time ever, it's Ben and not Solomon.

Not as ceremonious of a transition as he's imagined. He hasn't gotten to fire Doug yet, for instance.

But it's just as well. He's only been in charge for six months, and he hasn't wanted to make waves or make anyone feel nervous that ought to feel nervous. Ben wants the slip-ups to continue so that the hammer drop could have its full impact. But one drops before he has the chance.

Just now, he's called a meeting with Evan Bolinger, his Junior VP of Derivatives Management, once his contemporary that came up alongside the ranks with him when they were both lowly undergrad analysts.

Evan recently sent a scathing open letter to a New York newspaper slamming the Dvorak Group for their unethical practices. The double doors open tentatively and Evan shyly appears on the other side as his assistant closes them behind him.

Ben's intimidating good looks have only hardened with age, along with his innocence. Now that he's had his surgery, he barely walks with a limp, giving him the lumbering gait of a mob boss.

"Pull up a chair, Mr. Bolinger."

Evan respectfully takes a seat, wondering if he should be formal or fraternal with his new boss.

"My second time in the big office after all these years, and it's you," Evan sighs.

"Should've blown up your career last year, eh?" Ben replies with a grin, though Evan doesn't return it. He seems a bit nervous.

"Come on, Evan, there's no way you could think this was gonna end well."

"No, it's just... how's your dad?"

"My dad?"

"Sol— Mr. Dvorak."

"I know who my dad is," Ben answers curtly.

"I trust he won't be coming back?"

Ben maintains eye contact. "He has no plans to come back as of yet. I can't imagine why any of that matters."

"It's a big deal for everyone."

"Maybe," Ben shrugs. "It was bound to happen sooner or later."

"I suppose I was asking about *you* in a roundabout way. Doug talks."

Doug. The name makes him want to spit fire. Turns out he does indeed know where the bodies are buried so, for now, he stays.

"Doug is holding on by a thread of blackmail."

"Doug talks a lot. Says when he last spoke to Sol he sounded very confused," Evan expounds, sounding concerned.

Supposedly his investment shark days are over, but with Evan's blond and boyish looks, even after ten years, he's giving Ben the same psychopathic Howdy Doody routine he used to give clients. Ben doesn't flinch.

"Doug has not spoken to my father, he's a liar. Sol Dvorak is just taking a long, overdue vacation." Ben says it in a way so stoic that it could only be a lie. "Speaking of vacations..."

"Look, I'm not expecting to get my severance," Evan begins reasonably, "or the rest of my annual bonus, or any of the time, sweat and tears from the best years of my life that I gave."

"A smart man."

"I just want my stock."

Ben gives him a head shake. "Your stock is predicated on you completing your contract."

"Which I have."

"How do you figure?" Ben cocks his head.

"Ben... I've been here twelve years."

"And now you're quitting," Ben briefly raises his thick eye-brows.

"I'm entitled to at least five years' worth of stock."

"You didn't have stock options when you first started, Evan," Ben says, sitting back in his father's chair. "I didn't. No one did."

"Stop pointing that out, as if you were ever on the same level

3

as us," Evan sneers.

"You're right, I had *more* of a handicap. I *chose* to work my way up," Ben insists.

"My ass."

He shouldn't let the implication get to him, but he does. He's the boss now, as he would have always been. He didn't have to take the time to prove himself, but he did. The more he tried to earn his colleague's respect, the more they refused to give it. Jealous shits.

"You would've probably sucked my father's dick if you could trade places with me and skip every rung you had to climb."

"That's where you're wrong, Ben."

"You manage derivatives to make a difference, Evan?"

"I manage derivatives because I wanted to do *business*."

"You sure it wasn't because you wanted the prestige of putting The Dvorak Group on your premium stock business cards?"

"I could've easily gone to Morgan Stanley or Goldman Sachs."

"But you didn't. Maybe there, you couldn't overcharge your least knowledgable clients without reproach so easily?"

Evan sucks on his teeth. "Same thing happens everywhere and you know it."

"Problem is, the public thinks it only happens here. And that, Evan, is because of you. What would you have me do?"

"I'm the last one to play the martyr, you know that. But that's how bad it's gotten. Things have to change, Ben. I did what our Junior Management Directing cocksuckers told me, same as you. What was *your* excuse, choirboy? Had to live in the city off of $150K, did you?"

"My excuse is that I'm stuck here for eternity, and now I have a gambling problem," Ben replies, "only it's with other people's money and I fucking hate to lose."

"It doesn't have to *be* like this, Ben. Fucking teachers' retirements going up in smoke—"

"God*dammit*, Evan, that was six years ago! No one put a gun to your head."

"But no one stopped me! Why didn't anyone stop me?"

"Stop you? You fucking drank on that story for a year."

"I was trying to make it a win. But I couldn't. No one told me I couldn't escape it. No one told me the consequences."

"No one told you to grow a conscience midstream, Evan," Ben replies, trying to echo his father. "No one told you the consequences, because no one around here knows what they are."

"It's gotten worse if you can even imagine that. Remember what they taught us at Princeton, about subprime mortgages and we practically shit our pants? You should go down to our old offices, Ben. The analysts, fucking walking around calling the clients 'muppets.' While they're on the floor! The fuckin' hairless balls these kids have!"

"What's gotten into you?" Ben wonders.

"Nothing. Reality's gotten into me. Being able to go home and look into the eyes of my son, and tell him that his dad hasn't spent his life weaseling money out of good people. That's what's gotten into me."

Ben feels a strange twinge in his gut at his words.

"How is young Chester?"

"I wouldn't know. His mom won't let me see him. Says I ruined their lives when I sent the paper that story."

Ben sits stewing, thinking of what he should do. They have at least a month of bad press in front of them, and it doesn't matter who's been running the company for the last 30 years, Ben is in charge of it now. He can't throw his dad under the bus,

5

he has to take the heat.

He knows if his dad were still in charge, he'd have to make an example of Evan. He couldn't have the Dvorak Group leaking like a sieve. He couldn't just let him walk.

But his dad is a cunt, in the immutable words of his old friend.

"Look. I'll release a statement saying that we've terminated your employment, and offered you a fair severance package— along with a non-disclosure that you *will* agree to sign. No more singing, Mariah."

"Thank you, Mr. Dvorak."

"I can't give you your stock. Sorry, Evan. It's just not gonna happen."

Evan sat stonefaced before he replied, "Then you'll see me in court."

"And I'll agree to not grind you into a fine powder when you do— but only under the condition that you use that settlement money to reimburse those teachers."

Evan sighed and hung his head, knowing that he would never see that stock.

But Ben was offering him redemption, which might actually be better.

"How?" Evan wonders aloud. "Even if I win back every year's worth, I'll be lucky to get a fraction of what we owe them."

"What *you* owe them. And if you're looking to make some money fast, I may know a few investors..."

"Don't try and sell me, you bastard. I'll go with DG, but only if you handle it personally."

"Does it look like I'm still market-making?" Ben grins.

"You want my business or not, asshole?" Evan ribs him. Ben chuckles.

"Then we have a deal?" Ben extends an arm across the large

6

desk.

Evan extends his own arm after a few moments and the two shook hands. "Looks that way," Evan says.

"Excellent. You're fired."

"Thanks."

"I'll give Lisa the details. Meanwhile, clean out your shit."

"I've never been happier in my life, Ben. You should try it," says Evan, getting up from his chair.

"Not an option for me, unfortunately," Ben replies, resigned. "Remember that handicap I mentioned?"

"It's all just an illusion, Ben. Contracts, 'lockup' stock. Family names. They trained us to be slaves, trained us that the only way out was 'up,' but it never was. Sure, it was more money, but it's just more slavery. They want us to think like slaves, but we're not slaves, Ben. None of us are. Not yet."

* * *

Ben takes a cab ride to his apartment in the city after another long day of work. Still ruminating over his and Evan's conversation.

It's all just an illusion, he said.

Ben can't begin to understand what he could've possibly meant by that. Or why he thought such a notion would be helpful to a man like Ben, who did not have the luxury of walking away from his own family.

His older brother Grant had, but not without it practically killing him. He'd been the golden child, but it didn't matter to Grant. The more he was esteemed, the more he despised Dad for it.

After his brother's glaringly bad example, Ben's bar became

7

exceptionally low, so he supposed he could thank him for that. Though it has the annoying effect of turning Ben's accomplishments into a benchmark for how much more Grant could've done in the same position.

The cramps in his legs have become annoying, but not unbearable. Not even comparable. Eventually, he will have to break the promise to himself and have yet another surgery, which would bring the total to eight. His resolve is loosening, but he would still like to see how long he can go without breaking a single fucking promise.

He opens his apartment door, hangs up his keys, and leaves whatever isn't attached to him on the ground. When he gets to his bedroom his fiancée is standing there stark naked, her long black hair and her flawless, gold-kissed skin on display like an exclusive piece of art.

"Esmee?"

Her big black eyes are like saucers, searching his face for signs of elation.

"Three weeks in the Serengeti, and I still have my key. Are you proud of me?"

Ben knows he's expected to have some over the top reaction, but he can't muster it. He settles on perplexity and hopes it's enough.

"I thought you were in Israel until next month?"

"Nope. I'm here for the next month."

"You're here," he states the obvious.

"I'm here," she smiles.

For the briefest of moments, Ben realizes he hadn't missed her. The thought gives him alarm at first. But then he removes all his clothes, and promptly puts it out of his mind.

2

Present Day

B en rolls over in bed the next morning, Esmee still in a sleep coma beside him as she will be likely until the afternoon. He looks at her sleeping face and feels better. The smattering of freckles across Esmee's nose and cheeks reminds him that he only requires certain things as a man. And missing his fiancée when she was gone wasn't one of them. In fact, it might be an advantage.

He'd been in love once. If being "in love" meant missing someone when they were gone. And feeling their absence just as much as you could feel their presence. If he felt that with Esmee, their relationship would be unbearable, simply unsustainable. How is lack of crippling attachment a bad thing?

The way he's now seeing it, it's one less source of strain on the relationship, since they see each other so little. She has no intentions of slowing or settling down, which works just fine for him. He likes it about her that she's so ambitious and focused.

She's back in town for only a week or two, and they will likely see each other even less than usual, as it turns out that fashion models are quite busy. Naturally, as the unofficial president of the Dvorak Group, so is he.

Today, however, he is even busier, since his father Solomon's worsening condition now requires weekly meetings.

It doesn't, actually, if you ask him. But his older sister Valerie has taken over his care, and now it does.

After work, Ben makes the short trek to the lavish penthouse, once their family's home away from home while his father worked in the city (and his occasional whore haven they later found out). He greets his father's longtime maid Rosa and pours himself a cup of tea from the sterling silver set he was never allowed to touch growing up. One of many indulgences Ben allowed himself once the iron grip of his father's hand was finally vanquished.

"Let's get this over with," Ben says once Val makes her way downstairs, dressed in a fine business wool dress with leather boots.

"Grant's not going to make it," she sighs.

"Surprise."

"He says he can't find a place with good Wi-Fi."

"Even walking to the other side of his room and opening his laptop has become too much of a chore."

"Don't be too hard on him," Val says as she pours herself a cup of tea. "We're lucky he hasn't staged Dad's death. Besides, he's trying to really do that vow of silence thing."

As soon as Grant was old enough, he left the city to become a musician and later became a monk. Ben didn't even know they still made monks.

By the time Ben was old enough to decide to try his hand at the family business, his father's response was a tepid, "fine." Val was probably his second choice, but she went into politics, working to regulate the very investment banking firms that'd been run by their father's golfing buddies. The whole thing makes Ben wish he'd encouraged Val to play with dolls more.

"I tried to get more information out of his doctors. Apparently, Daddy hired lawyers, drew up some legalese to keep his prognosis confidential, even to himself. Unfortunately, they're not allowed to give us their professional opinion without legal action."

"Interesting."

"Isn't it?"

"Almost like he knows doctors are not to be trusted and will say anything to keep you bedridden and filling prescriptions."

"Now, now Ben. Not all doctors, you know that."

"Actually I don't. But that's really fucking interesting. That means he believed us, finally."

"Either that or simply didn't want to take the chance with his own health. Grandpa apparently died the same way, and it wasn't pretty."

"It's clearly Alzheimer's."

"Which reminds me, Ben, you should probably get tested to see if you have the same genetic markers."

"No thanks," Ben scoffs. "I think I'm more like the old man on that front."

"No one knows how much time he has left, but he certainly doesn't have enough time to wait for legal."

"He'll be dead by the time we get the records unsealed. Which would just reveal the same guessing game we're playing, more than likely. Everyone can see that. The old man knows— knew— what he was doing."

"I've been doing a lot of research. The symptoms seem to be around the '6 month' mark. But sometimes those symptoms go on for a while. It's oddly unpredictable."

Ben resents his father for developing Alzheimer's, one of the most all-consuming diseases that didn't even have the courtesy to leave its victims bedridden. His sister Valerie has all but dedicated herself to his care.

She spends every other day at the penthouse, playing nurse the same way she'd done with Ben all through his childhood. Her dedication seems genuine, a blessing that Benjamin knows his father has done nothing to deserve. Val is single-handedly keeping the vultures away from the shrewd businessman that spent his life amassing wealth and burning his bridges.

When Val found out their dad was essentially dying a slow, nihilistic death, she decided not to run for re-election, much to the dismay of her supporters in her district. Her reason for resigning remains a professional mystery hidden behind the industry stonewall that was "personal reasons."

"So Dad had a moment of clarity today," Val remembers as she walks into the study. Ben takes the cue to get up from the couch and follow her.

"I don't want to know."

"It was longer than five minutes."

"Then I really don't want to know."

"He seems to be out of the volatile anger phase. I think he understands what's happening to him."

Ben leans elegantly against the doorframe. "You've turned sentimental on me, Val. There's no way that's true. It's much more likely that we will all have to live with the consequences of his miserable life while he withers away in blissful ignorance."

"You do realize I've known you since birth, Benjamin? You can't fool me."

"I don't want to see him."

"Oh, believe me, I know," Val nods her head like an annoying

12

bird of paradise, her dull auburn hair in a long bob. Ben sighs as he changes the subject.

"Did you talk to the board?"

"I'm not going to talk to the board without you, you know that. Plus, Grant is going to stonewall. Dad would have to get up out of his rocker and recite the bylaws for him to agree to hand over his seats."

"You ever seen such a greedy monk in your life?"

"Can't say that I've ever seen a monk. Anyway, did you look at the financials yet?"

"For the quarter?"

"For the week. There was a check," she says with raised eyebrows. The eyebrows come back down and she stops as if her statement is meant to be revelatory.

"Well. That's quite the mystery, Nancy Drew."

"Be nice, or I won't tell you who it was from."

Now it's Ben's turn to raise a Dvorak's eyebrow. "Alright," he answers tentatively.

"Cynthia."

Ben sits stoically as if the name didn't ring a hundred bells.

"Gordon?" he confirms.

"Yes, genius, Cynthia Gordon."

Ben had to admit it was odd. But he could think of plenty of explanations.

Cynthia popped back up on his radar suddenly around five years ago as head of the design firm Indigo Properties. From there she went from a blip on his radar to an inescapable presence around town.

Her name went from a distant, private connotation to an enigmatic brand on everyone's lips. He never knew she could design homes or even wanted to, but he wasn't surprised. She tended to work hard, but she also had a creative streak. A tendency to stand out, take risks.

Her handiwork is sprouting up all around town, and it always puts a smile on his face. Even though he was technically supposed to hate her for what she did. Whatever that was.

Oddly, when he thinks about that relationship which is now a thousand years old and fossilized in romance, the betrayal is all but forgotten. He was young, she was even younger. She made a bad decision, and it looks as though she's learned from it. Of course, it could all be another one of her "scams."

Still. He is happy for her. He has no ill will towards her.

"Maybe she's done some work for the old man. Maybe he reached out years later, like the twisted bastard that he is, and commissioned her. Quietly. And... she... needed to pay him for... going over budget or... something," Ben reaches.

Okay, so maybe "plenty" explanations is a stretch.

"Not likely. See any Cynthia Gordon signatures around here? At the Scarsdale house?" Val persuasively argues. "And unless this check is six to nine months late, there's no way they've been in correspondence. She doesn't even know that he doesn't have the capacity to cash it himself."

"No one does. Outside of us. What's your point?"

Val gives him an airy laugh. She doesn't know the reaction she's expecting, but the fact that he's determined to make it out to be nothing is a little... odd.

"Would you like to know the amount?"

"Alright, Columbo, out with it."

"$139,000."

That gets his attention.

"Did it say what for?"

"I'm so glad you asked, because in the memo line was con-

14

spicuously written 'extortion + interest.'"

What the hell?

Ben is quiet, searching his mind, but there is no information there that can help him. According to his father, he'd been one of her "marks." It would be months before Ben was willing to entertain the idea. Solomon's tough love approach ensured that Ben would have to ruthlessly wipe away all traces of Cynthia from his soul or else. He succeeded, but at the cost of whatever respect he had left for the old man.

"Let me see it."

Val opens up her laptop on the desk as Ben comes to sit down at the large leather chair. The electronic copy of the check unexpectedly jolts his heart.

"Her handwriting, is it not?"

"Honestly, I don't know. I assume so," Ben replies, studying the loops in her signature, in the signing of their father's name, the last name he'd nearly given her.

"You never saw her write anything down, Benjamin?" Val scoffs, looming closely behind his chair.

"First time I'm ever seeing it," he says, stifling a smile. And yet, he intrinsically recognizes it.

There in the amount box is a total of $139,310.18

"An awfully specific amount of money, wouldn't you say?" Val says.

"I don't like what you're implying."

"I'm not implying anything. I'm saying the story's true," Val muttered. "She went to Dad for money, blackmailed him or something. Had some dirt on you, or him. He must've given it to her because now she's a big-time designer."

Ben can feel a blind rage coming up from the dark pit of his insides, but for some reason, by the time it can get to his heart it evaporates.

It isn't just that he doesn't want to believe it, it truly doesn't make sense to him.

He knows something happened. The way she was perp-walked out of the building, determined not to see him, was as fresh as the day it happened. If she was truly a criminal she would lay low and stay that way. Change her name. Not flaunt herself around town.

Some insidious cloud of guilt and shame and accusations made them both insist on avoiding each other like the plague. Even when her office is in Tribeca, and his office is in the same place it always was.

But he cannot concede the idea that she never cared. Even after ten years, he can't.

"She's only been at this design thing five years, Val, not ten. And she never mentioned anything about real estate or design. She was going to culinary school."

"Is that what she told you before or after you got undressed?"

"Why the hell would she lie about something like that?"

"I don't know, Ben. What else would she have to say to get close to us and take down the company?"

"Val, I'd have to seriously question your intelligence if you think that nonsense story has teeth. As if she could even do that."

"If you would've gone through with asking her to marry you, she could've taken us all down."

"Not really. Besides, the only person I told about that was you. And also, why would she give the money *back*?"

"...Guilty conscience?"

"Why would she have a guilty conscience if she was the vengeful, vindictive person Dad made her out to be? Since when

16

did Dad care about keeping vengeful vindictive people away from us, anyway?"

Ben asks for her benefit as well as his own. He chews a thumbnail. It seems as though today will be the day that he gets to the bottom of this, and he's not sure that he wants to.

"Cynth was different, Ben. She and her mom. They were peasants to Dad. Not the right kind of people. The family always came first."

"She was family to me. She was about to— become family..." Ben's voice trails off, his blood running cold. "Did *you* tell him?"

"That you wanted to propose to Cynth? No. Why would I care, I was knee-deep in campaign managing, remember? He figured it out eventually, I'm sure. Especially if his cronies were keeping him in the loop."

"No," Ben shakes his head, perusing his memory, "unless he had the apartment bugged there's no way they would've. Dad doesn't know shit about human relationships. And he didn't get to where he was by letting 20-year-olds get the kind of leverage to extort him. It's much more likely that he was extorting *her*, not the other way around."

"Extortion..." Val wonders aloud. "What could *Cynthia* possibly have that Dad didn't?"

The answer is obvious.

Him. The one thing she had, that Dad didn't, was him.

So maybe he *did* know about human relationships. Pity he couldn't have demonstrated it himself.

"Okay, so... let's say this check is the original amount he paid her, *plus* the interest. The going rate of interest ten years ago... probably around 7%," Ben filled in.

Ben opened the calculator on her laptop, plugging in the average rate of a business loan to a first time owner with decent

17

credit. He guessed at 100,000 being the sum. It was large enough to be tempting to a young girl with nothing, small and generic enough that his father could withdraw it without causing a stir.

That left a lot of interest. It had to be a full ten years worth. The exact amount of time since she'd left his life for good and refused to re-enter it, nearly to the day.

The amount came out to $39,310.18

"Fuck. *Fuck!*" Ben exclaimed. He got up and began to pace the room, gasping for breath.

"Ben, calm down."

"What the fuck is going on!"

"Ten years ago she started working at Dvorak Group."

"No, ten years ago she got *fired,* Val. She was just a kid. Fucking 20 years old. Not a mastermind!"

"Ten years interest on $100,000..." Val began, trying to piece together the puzzle. "I don't know, maybe she was a plant?"

"A cafeteria worker? No, if anyone screamed 'I'm a plant' it was Melanie, not Cynthia."

"Maybe... he bribed her to quit? Paid her to leave you alone?"

"Bring him in here. I want to talk to him. Right now."

"Ben, you know very well that won't do us a bit of good."

"He *fucked* me," Ben sneers. "Didn't I tell you? It was 100% him the entire time. I can't *believe* I ever listened to a word out of his mouth."

"If she left you for six figures, then he did you a favor. That's kind of worse than what we thought, isn't it?"

Ben thinks for a moment, the blind rage rising again. But it's snuffed out again, like before.

He shakes his head, a healthy trust growing for this feeling of his. "There's gotta be more to it."

"Ben. Don't go digging up skeletons, making them out to be

romance."

"What the hell did you show this to me for, if not to dig up skeletons?"

"To show you that Cynthia was bad news. Is *still* bad news. They were obviously in some kind of cahoots. I thought after ten years, you wouldn't still have stars in your eyes."

"Maybe I *liked* the stars, Val. I was a kid too, I was allowed to have them. Maybe I just don't appreciate that my fucking father *paid* to have those stars forcibly *removed*."

"Does it have to be this Romeo and Juliet scenario? Although, I have to say it's rather touching. I didn't know there was still a romantic in there."

"I certainly don't believe that dogshit story Dad told me anymore."

"Yeah, but comic book villain isn't Dad's style either. It was always a slight omission of the truth that did the most damage."

"She never betrayed me. Or, I don't know. Maybe she did but... she never *forgot*."

Extortion + interest, the memo read. Ben smiled, a warmth coming over him for the first time in a long time.

Cynthia. She's probably made it her life's mission to pay that money back. He was never angry at her, but it was finally starting to make sense.

But now he has a frightening possibility in front of him— contacting her for the first time in ten years.

He's never felt so pukey about the prospect, and that was saying something. But he suddenly has more courage than he ever had to do it. If he couldn't find absolution, he could at least find answers.

"Well, I know I'm not going to be able to stop you from doing whatever you're about to do, but just be careful, Ben. You're the de facto CEO of the company now. You can't afford to be naive about saboteurs."

"The only saboteur is upstairs shitting himself right now. And I don't have to worry about him. Not anymore."

3

Present Day

"So, I finally wrote that *ba-jon* deh check, Mom."

Cynthia Gordon finally speaks after sitting wordlessly at her mother's grave for a few minutes, her sleek dark hair whipping about her face in the wind. She tames it with her smooth fingers, her rich light brown skin like a pleasant, permanent tan.

She changes the old roses out for the fresh flowers she brought, this time orange lilies, brilliant and stark against the cold gray of her mother's burial stone.

"$139, 310. And 18 fool cent. How yuh like 'dat, eh?" she smiles. "I know I could've done it earlier, but. I wasn't about to put the business in jeopardy just to give some old white man the finger. He makes that in an hour. But *me*, Mama. Would you have ever imagined?"

She chuckles a bit, her blue-gray eyes shiny with memories.

"Of course you did. I always imagined doing it in person though, y'enuh? Go right up to the top floor of that building an' give 'em deh lengt' ah mih *tongue*. I even had a little speech ready: 'Hey, asshole, thanks for the loan. I know yuh meant it

21

for *evil*, I know yuh took me fuh *dotish*, enuh?'" Cynthia speaks in her mother's Grenadian patois, Cynthia's last familial link to it now buried.

"'So here's every cent of it back, plus interest.' But then the day came and... I couldn't do it. Every time I go into the city, it makes me sick to even go past there. I even saw Benji once or twice," she confessed, distracted for a moment. "First time it was like lookin' a *jumbie*. Saw that *kilketay* walk a' his, and fuh true, I almost did a *catspraddle* right *smack* in deh *street,* enuh. Started stalkin' him online a likkle bit after that, enuh. He looks good. Engaged. *Again.* He was in the news the other day. I guess the boss man is getting ready to retire."

Cynthia feels a now-familiar ache when she thinks of the criminally attractive, well-to-do, not-quite-boyfriend of her youth. Pure puppy love. What her classmates lived for on the Jersey Shore in the summers. But it was much more than any of her classmates would've dreamed up for themselves.

At the time, she considered it compensation for missing out on the class trip, on freshman year at college, all the milestones she'd childishly looked forward to, back then. Maybe that's why she threw caution to the wind like she never had, and likely never will again. She was making up for the time she thought she lost. A lot of good it did her.

No, she shouldn't say that. Not like that. *Take it back,* she thought to herself.

"Anyway, it's done. '*Dead up,*' Daddy would say. I don't owe that family a damn thing anymore. That sure was a beautiful house we bought though, wasn't it? Even when it was a piece of shit. Seems like a million years ago."

The wind blows her tears sideways before they can fall.

"Well. I should go, I'm up to my eyeballs in deadlines, Mama.

I know I haven't been able to visit like I used to. I'm sorry about that. I'll try to be back next week, okay?"

Cynthia leaves her mother's side, reluctantly to leave her where she lay in the cold ground. She always hated being outside in the cold.

Thankfully her current project is close by. When she pulls up, just looking at it causes her to groan, though it is beautiful. But like any bad headache, the pain starts to make you wonder why you value anything.

She looks at the muddy front yard in dismay. From the looks of it, the big reveal is officially going to be delayed by at least 30 days. She rubs her worried forehead.

She gets out of her car and her project manager Gabe is already anticipating her mood.

"It's further along than it looks, I promise."

"I hate being behind schedule, Gabe. That's why I hired you, Gabe."

"I know."

"It's why I became a realtor, so I wouldn't have to wait on a fucking realtor. It's why I let you talk me into completely canceling out that decision by then hiring my *own* realtors. Gabe. So I could just focus on design, get selective with our projects. And then we could catch up. Isn't that what you said? Gabe?"

"Okay, first of all, thank you for giving me the credit for single-handedly turning you into a prominent, in-demand, full-time designer. Secondly, watching you work your fingers to the bone when you could be handing those things off to someone else is my personal pet peeve, and you know that."

"But ah get it *done*, Dan. Dat's why *ah* like t'be doin' it, enuh. Lef tuh me, dis one set 'ah lazy man wuk ends *now* fuh now," Cynthia remarks in a rare island creole that Gabe was starting

23

to understand more and more.

It doesn't matter what she's saying. Its presence means she's in the mood to fire someone.

She follows him inside, where the cabinets that are primed for paint and trim soothe her panic.

"How? Hooowww, Gabe. Today was supposed to be open house, did you know that?"

"It all started with the countertops."

"The damn countertops," she laments, "I mean, it was a week delay. It was harmless."

"Well, then it rained."

"The fuckin' rain. The rain is to blame."

"If we'd have just gotten the Carerra marble, we'd be on time. Early even."

Cynthia lays herself on top of the gold Calacatta countertop with her hands outstretched, as if it's a dinosaur at Jurassic Park. Gabe just laughs.

"Gabe, what am I doing wrong that I can't seem to catch up? We left plenty of room for contingencies."

"Perhaps we should stop doing that," her project manager suggests.

"I like the way you think, Gabriel. Next time, we make these fuckers deliver our shit on time, or else they don't get paid and I'm sending you to IKEA."

"Sound like a plan to me, boss."

"Did we close on the Moss property?" she asks as she surveys the dining room.

"Still waiting on the final inspection to come back."

Cynthia gives a slow turn towards Gabe as though in disbelief.

"They should've just used our guy."

"They should've used our guy."

"This is going to be a shit show. I'm gonna see if Shelly can call the engineer, start pulling permits as soon as they call us back and tell us it's a no-go. Which they *will* do. I can't afford more than a two-week delay on this as it is."

"I told you anything other than a cash buy was going to be a nightmare."

"I don't care, I want this house."

"Since when do you get emotional about a buy?"

"Since I can afford to. It's not every day you find your dream house."

"I think you mean 'soon-to-be-someone-else's' dream house."

"Semantics."

"I honestly don't see what's so dreamy about it. The thing is sinking, and it has the tiniest, most unfunctional kitchen I've ever seen. We're probably going to lose money it."

"We won't. It has a carport."

"You're lucky it's just outside the historical district. It's a municipal nightmare as it is. And it's ugly."

"Gabe, it has a goddamned carport. Honestly, it's like you don't even hear me when I talk."

"You got it for next to nothing, and you still paid too much. Did I mention it's ugly?"

"Gabe, you are a practical realist, and a champion with planning and punctuality. I think we should continue speaking two separate languages with each other. It builds character."

"I've never seen someone get so wrapped up in a property when designing them. Honestly, I don't think it's good for you. I'd tell you to get formal training again, but I doubt you'll listen to me."

"Lots of people with formal training never get to where I am."

Suddenly she notices her assistant calling.

"Caira, what's up?"

"You just got a call from a potential client."

"Caira, you know we're not taking private design jobs right now."

"Well... that's why I called. He's not taking no for an answer."

Cynthia's heart skips a beat.

There aren't a lot of men left these days who aren't taking no for an answer. And she only knows one.

Sol Dvorak kept tabs on Cynthia in the first few years. He sent a gift when Indigo Properties opened, a thinly veiled threat of a gesture. A large bouquet of flowers when her mother died signaled to her that there was nothing that happened that he didn't know about.

He's obviously received her check.

"Is it the Dvorak Group?"

"How'd you know?"

"Was it him or his office?"

"It was Mr. Dvorak. He says it's for his personal residence."

Oh no.

"Solomon Dvorak wants me to *design* for him?"

"No, it's the son."

Oh no. Oh *hell* no.

Maybe it's not Benji, maybe it's... Grant.

"The perpetually engaged one?"

"Yes."

"Shit," Cynthia closes her eyes.

Benji?? Since when is he privy to his father's private correspondence?!

"Tell him we politely decline."

"Tell him what?!" her project manager furrows his brow,

26

looking at her with dismay. Cynthia makes a habit of running all her jobs by Gabe, but this one she simply isn't willing to take.

He's already heard the name. He isn't going to be happy.

"You want me to tell Benjamin Dvorak that we decline his business?" Caira confirms, politely implying that her boss might be insane.

"Yes, Caira, I do. No means no. We're not taking private design jobs right now."

"Hold on... you know more than one Dvorak? Personally??" Gabe marvels.

Cynthia put Caira on speakerphone so that she wouldn't have to repeat herself.

"Caira, you there?"

"Yes, ma'am."

"Is he waiting for your response?"

"I told him I would contact you personally and then get back to him."

"Did he tell you any of the specs?"

"It's in Scarsdale. 3,100 square feet, he wants the kitchen and all the bathrooms done."

"What year was it built?"

"Dunno, but the subdivision is less than 5 years old."

"Okay. Tell him, that it will be at least a year before we can fit him in."

"Cynth," Gabe looks at her in disbelief.

"What if he doesn't accept that?"

"He has no choice."

"Okay... but what if he doesn't?"

Caira's demeanor is bringing back all the disgusting feelings she felt being at the Dvorak Group. They're the type of family that gets whatever they want. They were ruthlessly privileged.

She doesn't know how closely Ben is following in his father's footsteps, but she does know that he would eventually find a way to get what he wanted. Wouldn't have to sweat, threaten, or even raise his voice. All he'd have to do was pay some money. If that didn't work, then he'd find whatever it is you cared about— buy him, her, or it— and hold that over your head to get it.

Cynthia knows she risked a run-in with someone, paying that money back. She doesn't know what to make of Ben contacting her instead of Sol. He seems to have figured out something about the deal.

And, of course, he would take his sudden discovery to instantly mean that she wanted him to start contacting her out of the blue and bothering her. Because, of course, that's what everyone wanted, right?

He's flaunted his international women of color in her face for the past five-ish years. Cynthia tries to take it in stride— considers it a form of flattery even— but part of her is pretty sure he's trying to ingratiate her with his life decisions.

And now, the first time he reaches out to her in a decade, he wants her to design for him and his fiancee's love nest?? The notion is slowly eroding her afternoon.

"If he still doesn't take no for an answer, tell him I require a half-million dollar inconvenience fee."

"Holy shit, Cynth what is your deal??"

"My deal is that I meant what I said about no new clients. These rich types aren't used to hearing the word 'no' and they think they can buy the world. So that's my price."

"Okey-doke," Caira says apprehensively before hanging up.

"They sure put a bee in your bonnet," Gabe says, referring to her previous work history.

"I wasn't there long enough for all that, but let's just say I saw

28

enough."

* * *

Benjamin Dvorak stares at Cynthia Gordon's business card, the one he received from his senior VP after she rehabbed their home.

"Hold all my calls," he tells his assistant. He flips the thick ply in his hands and thumbs the name across the top for twenty minutes.

He doesn't mean to stare at it so long. But he's scared to call the number.

The last time he saw her they hadn't spoken. Back when he was still an analyst and starting his MBA. He was coming back from an early lunch with some colleagues (which he never takes) off-campus (which never happens, to this day).

He saw her being escorted out as he was coming in. She looked so guilty it was like looking at a completely different person. Wouldn't even look him in the eye. They kept a low profile on their relationship, so it wasn't like he could grab her and demand she tell him what was happening. Nor did he know they would never lay eyes on each other again after that moment.

Only later had his father told him of her supposedly elaborate vendetta against the Dvorak Group for what happened to her family during the financial crisis. Apparently, Cynthia blamed them for what happened to her family after her mother lost everything and became solvent.

He didn't want to believe it at first, because it seemed so unbelievable to him at the time. But he couldn't deny it explained a number of things. Such as her Disney princess-like elusiveness. She knew how to make you feel like she was your friend without

29

realizing how little you actually knew of her.

She dodged it masterfully. So much so, that Ben's gut didn't object when his father told him a lie.

Her silence after that day was deafening, her disappearance as damning as it was cold. He'd returned to his apartment to find most of her things gone, besides a bottle of pink hair dye, her work uniform, and his key.

He became a wreck. His engagement to Melanie ended bitterly and he worked like a madman. And when she re-appeared years later, reinvented, their circles unbearably close, he had to concede that she'd obviously come into some kind of windfall to get to where she was with virtually no connections.

Still, he could never make her fully guilty in his mind. He started to think perhaps her elaborate con only started that way. Perhaps she developed real feelings that she hadn't meant to. He thinks of the late nights that melted into dawn, and the not-so-innocent interludes between shifts as he twirled the card around his fingertips.

After ten years he has the chance to know what happened once and for all. He takes a deep breath as he picks up the receiver in his office and dials, saying goodbye to his pre-phone call ignorance.

"Indigo Properties, this is Jeanine?"

"Yes, this is..." he hesitates.

He doesn't want to reveal his name to anyone but Cynthia herself. Besides, what if he's on some kind of no-call list?

"I don't suppose there's a way I could speak to Cynthia Gordon directly."

"I can put you through to her assistant if this is regarding an existing project."

An existing project. Hm.

Maybe a legitimate reason to call would help alleviate his jitters. His property in Scarsdale could use some attention.

Esmee would adore Cynthia. And Esmee couldn't fault him for having a legitimate reason to lay eyes on her.

"Actually, I'm an old friend. We haven't been in touch in years and I'm looking to get some work done on a property of mine. I was referred to her by one of her clients."

"I'm almost sure she's not taking on any new clients, but I'll put you through to Caira."

Caira confirms Jeanine's suspicions. Thoroughly.

"Miss Gordon has a pretty extensive waiting list, Mr. Dvorak."

"Is there a way I can speak to her directly? We're actually old friends."

"Yes, you've said that."

Ben smiles. Seems like she's got a good group of people around her.

"You don't believe me?"

"With all due respect, Mr. Dvorak, you could be anyone. From what I know of Miss Gordon, her 'old friends' don't typically use her general business line to get in touch with her."

Ben sits back in his office chair overlooking his 180-degree view of the skyline. "Caira, is it?"

"Yes, sir."

"I can tell you're very good at your job, Caira. I'm 100% sure that your boss is very busy, and you're doing a very good job fielding her phone calls. I am equally 100% sure, that if it wasn't for my name, I would've probably had to settle for leaving a message with the receptionist.

"I've known access my entire life. The only reason that I don't already have your boss's number is that I fucked up, many years ago. And I didn't even know. In fact, I just found out today. So,

31

Caira, if you were to get in touch with her right now on my behalf, and tell her who's calling, at the very least, I guarantee you, you will not be reprimanded.

"*But*, if I get in touch with her some other way, and just so happen to mention the assistant who didn't believe it was me calling, well..." Ben trails off, letting Caira fill in the consequences herself.

He knows that in real life he doesn't have a leg to stand on. In real life, Caira is his only hope. And if Cynthia ever found out that Caira told him he could go fuck himself, she'd probably give her a raise. But his persuasive speech wins out.

"...If you don't mind waiting, Mr. Dvorak, I'll try her right now."

"Please," he says.

His heart thunders, as though Caira is going to come back with Cynthia on three-way like they're all a bunch of teenagers. Knowing now that his father blackmailed her, he couldn't be sure of himself at all. His moral high ground is crumbling under his feet.

Maybe he should've left it all behind to go find her.

He didn't know the old man had given her money. They could've cashed that check, he could've cleaned out every secret stash of money he had, and they could've traveled the world until they used every cent— he, Cynthia, and her lovely mom, Bev.

She could've found work in some of the greatest restaurants in France, Italy, Brussels. He could've... cleaned toilets, stacked bricks. Went to bed every night sore and exhausted after a day of honest work. She could've taught him how to be poor.

There was something about manual labor that almost frightened him somewhere deep down. He still had a long list of fears to overcome, what with his mother constantly hovering over him, bug-eyed, assuring him of what he would never be able to do, parroting the doctors like there was an honorary degree in it for her.

But with Cynthia next to him, he could've found the courage. He would've done anything to take care of her. He should've protected her.

But then if he'd done that, he would've had her. And he doesn't deserve her. Especially not now.

A minute later, Caira returns with much lower optimism in her voice.

"I was able to get in touch with Miss Gordon, but unfortunately she was adamant about not taking any new business."

"Did you tell her who was calling?"

"I did."

"And what did she say?"

"She said to tell you that we politely decline."

Ben can't stop the smile spreading across his face.

"Did she sound angry?"

"Um... she sounded... resolute."

He smiles even wider, picturing it. All these years of silence. And now there is a mere assistant separating them.

"Can you tell her that I won't take 'no' for an answer?"

"She said you would say that, and to tell you that she requires a $500,000 inconvenience fee upfront, sir," Caira responds, adding the "upfront." She's curious about this "old friend." The boss has been holding out on them, it seems.

"I see," Ben chuckles a bit. "Well. At least that isn't a 'no,' isn't that right, Caira?"

"An excellent outlook, Mr. Dvorak," Caira replies.

Ben smiles. It seems Cynthia really does only speak in zeroes.

He didn't remember that about her.

"Tell her I will consider her offer. By the way, when will Miss Gordon be done with her current project?"

"I don't know, sir, but I can tell you she is a bit behind schedule and has several rehab projects in the pipeline."

After Ben hangs up his pleasant phone call with Cynthia's assistant, he summons his own via intercom.

"Get me Barrett on the line."

Not a moment later his office phone is ringing again.

"Barrett. How easy would it be to find out what Indigo Properties is acquiring next? Great. I need you to do some detective work."

* * *

After three weeks of delay, Cynthia is posting the "Open House" sign in front of the finally finished current project. Gabe shows up to the open house looking as though he's about to tell Cynthia something very very bad.

"Who died?" Cynthia asks.

"Hopefully no one," Gabe responds. "Certainly not the messenger."

"Gaaabe," she whines. "It's a gorgeous day for showing a property. Why are you bringing me bad news?"

"The Moss property. The deal fell through."

Cynthia hangs her head.

"How long have you known?"

"Caira just told me."

"Because she was afraid to tell *me*."

"Precisely."

Cynthia takes a deep breath and lets it seep out into a growing groan of frustration.

"What the hell happened?"

"They went with another buyer."

"We had a contract!"

"The buyer offered to cover their legal fees if necessary."

Cynthia went cold.

"Did this buyer happen to have the last name Dvorak?"

"...I'll find out," Gabe furrows his brow.

But Cynthia already knows the answer.

He'll find out what you love and hang it over your head.

She looks down at her buzzing phone. It's Caira.

"Boss, I have an update that's... sorta good, actually, in a way. Did Gabe tell you... the news?"

"You're about to tell me that Ben Dvorak bought the Moss property and he wants me to design it."

"That's... yeah. How'd you know that?"

Cynthia rolls her eyes.

"Call it a hunch."

4

Ten Years Ago

Cynthia heard the alarm go off inside the back of the van. She looked around for signs of her mother, but she was already gone. Probably already in the shower at the rec center where they were parked.

Cynthia was hoping to have time to wash the dark purple out of her hair and give it a break. Even though her wavy, silky-textured curls were under a hair net and hat most of the day, they were giving her a hard time at work about her hair dyeing obsession.

But it was the cheapest thing she could regularly do to re-invent herself. After being homeless for 14 months, she found something that could remind her that there were still some things left in life she could control, that not all drastic changes were negative. It oddly kept her sane.

Cynthia stretched as she usually did after sleeping in the cramped, albeit spacious stow n' go floor of the minivan that'd become their permanent home since May of last year.

Cynthia's mother Bev had weathered what could only be described as the perfect storm. The financial crisis that triggered a recession hit the Gordon family right in the gonads, at the time they needed it the least.

Thousands were laid off at the manufacturing plant, including Bev, who'd been there 20 years and was looking forward to retirement. This was right around the time she discovered that her house was practically worthless.

It didn't matter to her, she would've stayed in it forever. She loved that house. But it'd been exactly 5 years since she'd bought the house with no money down, an opportunity that was an absolute blessing from God, at the time. But then the adjustable rate kicked in, and her payment doubled.

She had to give it back. She tried to, anyway. The bank refused until her loan defaulted.

Now Bev was 50 years old without a degree and virtually un-hireable. She had a lofty goal to go back to school, finish her degree, and hopefully get back on her feet by the end of the year. She wouldn't be able to buy another house with her credit in the state it was now in, nor could she afford to rent in the district in which Cynthia went to school.

Never in her life did Bev ever set out to be homeless. It just... happened.

Cynthia thought it wasn't all bad, really. In some ways, it was freeing. A year later, however, they'd worn out every friend or family member favor they could call in, and disillusionment was setting in. People wanted to do more help, but the recession ensured that everyone had their own problems to deal with.

Cynthia started working soon after high school and they found themselves in Jersey City, where it was easier to get around unbothered by the cops. They showered at the YMCA, slept in secured parking lots, and ate anywhere there was free Wi-Fi. Both the girls worked temp jobs and made enough to pay what it cost to be homeless in New Jersey. What they had saved up, they just had to spend on a new transmission for the van, their current home, and their needed source of transportation when they weren't in the city. It was only July, but winter weather would soon be upon them, and without their savings, they might be "moving" to Florida.

The only silver lining was Bev's degree, now only one semester away. If she could get a decent job, they could save up enough to afford a one-bedroom apartment in a month or two. Bev felt terrible about the fact that Cynthia would have to continue to work in order for them to afford to live in the places they wanted. She should be in college.

But Cynthia was a trooper. For some reason, she liked to be on her feet all day. Waitressing, fast food, she did every grunt job she could find. She figured since culinary school was now indefinitely postponed, she wanted to get as close as she could, with experience as relevant as she could manage.

Today was free pancake day at IHOP, so they went there for breakfast, and would likely be back for lunch as well as dinner.

Bev looked across the table at her daughter's perplexing hair color and vowed to say nothing. Aside from their light brown hue, Bev hardly resembled her daughter now, who inherited her late husband's light eyes and symmetrical features. Bev had fine black hair and thick brows, putting the "Indian" in West Indian. Cynthia began over a three stack.

"So, I told you about Jorge leaving the steakhouse right?"

"Deh manager dat likes you? Ah t'ought he was already gone?"

"No, he turned in his notice but he's got a few days left. Well, he wants me to come with him."

"Come wit 'im whey?"

"To this job he's going to. He says they're looking for cooks

38

and he put in a good word for me."

"Is so? Well now, dat's awfully nice a' him," Bev said skeptically, "is he... expecting su'm in return?"

"I don't think so. But he knows that I want to run my own restaurant one day and that I can't afford culinary school right now. He says the place is so short-staffed, they might take a chance on me, even if I don't have the experience."

"Yuh haven't been atta steakhouse very long, Cynti, and yuh doing pretty good. Don't get yuh work history in some *bachanal* trailin' a 'ting, enuh."

"It's not that big of a deal to employers these days, Mama, not at the beginning. Besides, they're hiring him to run the kitchen, so he's only gonna put me right where I want to be."

"Well, if dat's deh case... it sounds like just deh opportunity yuh need."

"Did I mention they're gonna pay me a dollar more?"

"No, yuh didn't. Yuh shoulda opened wi'dat, gyal."

"Had to jump on that."

"Yuh be makin' more dan ah, at dis point."

"They might even let me take home leftovers at this place. Save us a ton on meals."

"Whey's 'dis place?"

"It's this swanky place downtown. It's not even a restaurant, it's a cafeteria inside of a financial building. The Dvorak group."

"Dvorak group?"

"Yeah. You heard of it?"

"Sure. At work, Dvorak had deir hands in all kinds a' companies. I t'ink dey deh reason ah got laid off."

"Oh. Well, I don't have to take the job."

"Don' be silly. D'ese companies get *eaten* by bigger companies an' visa versa, anyway. It's nutting personal."

"If you can name names, I might be able to whip up something disgusting," Cynthia suggested.

Bev laughed, her signature smile lighting up her black eyes and face.

"Doh beat up, Cynt'ya," her mom shook her head. "But people *choke* every day, enuh?"

Cynthia huffed a laugh with her mouth full of pancake. She took a swig of coffee.

"I know."

* * *

On Cynthia's first day her new manager Jorge showed everyone the ropes.

"As some of you know, this is my first day. And it's some of yours too," Jorge directed at Cynthia with a wink. "Give us newbies time to learn this kitchen. For now, I'm handing the reins over to Virginia."

Jorge took a step back and the timid older woman on the end spoke up in a shy voice.

"I've been here a little over five years now, which makes me the veteran, I guess," Virginia began. "The previous manager had worked here for twelve years. But he had a family emergency. Basically, as long as you remember to write down what you do before you do it on the chart back here, you'll do fine. Train yourself as early as possible to write everything down."

Jorge went on a little longer before Virginia put her hand up shyly in the corner again. It seemed her newfound spotlight had sparked a few more ideas.

"Really quick, I just remembered that there was one major rule that David, our old manager used to always emphasize, and that was 'no fraternizing with employees.' A lot of these guys, they're young, fresh out of college, and they look like your friends or someone you went to school with, but they're not. They're stockbrokers and investment bankers. They're cute and young, and they'll try to flirt with you. Some of you ladies, I can already tell there's gonna be some trouble," she said, laughing it off.

The room giggled a bit but she was obviously serious. She looked over at Cynthia when she began the sentence.

"Just do yourself a favor and stay in the kitchen, near the kitchen as much as you can. Even if they flirt with you and talk to you, be nice, but don't encourage them. I'm saying this for you, not for them. Because it's not gonna end bad for them, it'll only be bad for you. One of them is the son of the owner of this place. Benjamin Dvorak. He's very nice, very down to Earth, but don't be fooled. You do not want to get caught up with any of these people."

The advice struck everyone as a bit old-fashioned, but it was coming from an elderly woman named Virginia, so they understood. Besides, she seemed to be speaking from experience. A few of the guys seemed to scoff at it, and Cynthia couldn't tell if that meant that they thought the girls they worked with weren't all that, or that stockbrokers weren't. Jorge seemed to appreciate her making a speech that he would not, at this point, be comfortable making.

Cynthia stayed in the back for her first day, doing lunch service and prepping for tomorrow.

"You work so fast, Cynthia," Jorge marveled. "Having you here is going to save my ass."

"You don't need me, you're doing a great job."

"I don't think I earned very much respect this morning."

41

"Are you kidding? Anyone that didn't appreciate you giving Virginia props today can get fired," Cynthia assured him.

"She turned out to be... very opinionated."

"Not so shy when it came to the sex talk."

"I can only imagine what she's already seen working here."

"The sheer tomfoolery," Cynthia gossiped. "You know she looked straight at me when she started talking."

Jorge laughed. "So, I'm thinking about incorporating some of the food we did at the steakhouse. You still remember the chicken fried steak?"

"I remember that it killed me to put all that bouillon in the gravy every day."

"Yeah, about that. I was thinking we're free to make tweaks however we want."

Cynthia pointed at him with a smile in her eyes. "Now you're speaking my language."

"Got any other recipes that are easy for feeding armies and that anyone can replicate?"

Cynthia's gray-blue irises sparkled as she downplayed her enthusiasm. "I can think of a few."

"Oh and by the way... speaking of Virginia's impassioned warning earlier..."

"Yeah?" Cynthia smirked.

"Just remember that whatever you do reflects on me."

She furrowed her brow. "What's that supposed to mean?"

"I'm just saying, Cynthia. You're young. Beautiful."

"Also, black and poor and not anyone's type who works in a place like this. And vice versa," she argued.

"Honestly, I think Virginia was probably downplaying it. These rich boy types... people like us, we're disposable to them."

"You must really think I'm some kind of sucker."

"I'm just being protective. I know I'm firmly in the friend zone—"

"Jorge..."

He gave her a look that stopped her from going further.

"As I was saying, I'm in the friend zone, and that's fine because we work together. Believe it or not, I'd much rather have you on my team. You're young and too pretty to be working in a kitchen. You might as well hear it now because you're about to hear it a hundred more times."

"We weren't even allowed to take outside tips from customers at the steakhouse. You think I don't know what it means to stay out of trouble?"

"It's not as easy as all that. I'm just saying. If, for whatever reason, it can't be avoided... just be careful."

"You have my word, Jorge, that I will clock in every day, do my job, and then kindly leave."

Not an hour later, Cynthia was eating her words. Because the moment she noticed Ben smoking a cigarette near the service entrance, she nearly lost her breath.

He looked to be a little older, the senior to her freshman. He was on crutches, those state of the art ones that cuff around the arm and have handles halfway down. He'd shed them and stacked them up against the concrete building, as though he didn't really need them.

He wore the same uniform as the other young men at work: a crisp, white dress shirt and slacks. But he didn't look like the others, who were all auditioning to be the lead in American Psycho.

He probably couldn't even rent a car but already the clothes weren't wearing *him*. He was that kind of fine that looked like it was from a bygone era, but would never not be sexy. Like some handsome ghost, some strange hormonal manifestation from the distant past come to test her resolve to not lose focus.

He returned himself to the crutches and it was the first time she saw his exaggerated gait, his calf and thigh muscles turned inward, the soles of his shoes lifted off the ground. He was tall, despite his bowed appearance. There was nothing diminutive or apologetic in his walk, as if daring you to perceive it as anything but normal.

Her inner voice gasped. She was instantly tamping down her imagination and curiosity. What does a disabled guy do to make himself *that* sexy?

Maybe there's a chance that every other woman in the world was too shallow to share her opinion, and she could have him with virtually no competition. Ever. He had to be loaded to be working at a place like this. If not now, then he will be.

If she hadn't ducked behind a wall before she could get a good look at his deep-set brown eyes, the same color as his dark hair, she may have never looked away.

His shirt sleeves were unbuttoned and rolled up, as though in the midst of a long workday that showed no signs of being over. She was just able to drink in the sight of him taking the last drag of his cigarette before he retreated back inside. She took a deep breath and shook her head when the coast was clear.

"Shit," she exclaimed as if remembering something foreboding. She could only hope and pray that she wasn't his type. But if Virginia's impassioned speech was any indication, she didn't stand a chance.

* * *

"So, I know you were wondering, I aced my interview today,"

Melanie began.

"That's great, honey," Ben said absentmindedly over the phone, using his break time to return his fiancee's call.

Melanie was in law school, about to become a paralegal at a prestigious firm not far from the Dvorak building. Her father was an investor friend of the family who had a fortune in natural resources. They had been dating since junior year.

"I won't go into it now, I know you're busy. I'll regale the tale at dinner so everyone can hear it all at once."

Ben rubbed his soft fingers across his mouth. "...Oh shit, was that tonight?"

"Tomorrow," Melanie gave a disappointed sigh. "Don't tell me you have to work."

"Probably. The guys haven't even started on this pitch book, I doubt it'll be done by tomorrow."

"Ben, you're still pulling all-nighters, working 100 hours a week? Surely, you can get out of it."

"Well... I'm sure I could, but the guys need me. Their dad isn't the owner."

"Ben, anyone who's still bringing up who you are and who you're related to, after three years, can go fuck themselves. You're playing by the rules, even for a Princeton graduate. And as much as I admire you for it, we've been planning this for weeks. I worked around your little job stipulations and scheduled it in advance. Your own father is going to be at this dinner, Benjamin."

"My father isn't a 2nd tier analyst. But you know what my schedule's like."

"You're gonna be these guys' bosses eventually, whether you cut out for Sunday dinner or not."

"All the more reason to prove myself," Ben insisted. "If not

45

to them, to me."

Melanie rubbed her forehead wordlessly, reminding herself that she only had to deal with this strange pseudo-ambition of his for a few years. And after that, it would all be dinner parties and rubbing shoulders, and using Dvorak connections to get things done.

She liked that he still wanted to be a boy scout at this age, probably a moral side effect of being born a cripple. Slows down the inevitable progression into permanent asshole status, like their fathers. She might even be able to love their children.

Still. Eventually, he would need to become that asshole. The fact that he couldn't just take the advantageous hand that was dealt him and be happy with it was pretty annoying. If he was trying to be like a poor person, he was insulting them with his insistence on always having a choice.

"If you didn't always insist on trying to survive on that paltry salary, you could be closer to me on the upper east side."

"$140K is not paltry to most people, Mel," Ben smiled.

"It is to New Yorkers, and you know it. Especially if they work as much as you. You're basically making as much as a butcher."

"Are we honestly going to have this conversation every time we talk?"

"No. Just when you cancel on me. We've already postponed this dinner twice. I can't cancel again, Benjamin," Melanie warned.

He was pretty sure if he came waltzing into dinner drunk off his ass, pissed inside of whatever protein they were having, announced that the marriage was off and that he was quitting, Melanie would just laugh nervously, her parents a little less so, and his father would forcefully tell him to sit down with only a look.

"Don't cancel," he instructed her. "I'll do my best, but like I said I can't give you a definite either way."

"You know, two people in a committed relationship need to spend at least 2.3 hours together daily to realistically beat the statistics of divorce."

"Well, we're not married yet," he smirked. "Once I get the MBA things will be different, I promise. All due respect, Melanie, you knew what the job was."

"I did," was Melanie's level headed response. "But we also agreed not to let work encroach on the relationship. We need to start making time for each other."

A distant part of him was always screaming *Get out. Now.* He didn't know whether to trust this voice, but every time Melanie used the term "relationship" and "we agreed" that voice got a little louder.

But he was too far in with Melanie. She knew and accepted everything about him, understood the bizarre confinement of prominent families. The sex was wild. He was glad of that. As a young man, he was certain that was all he would ever need if he had to marry Melanie to appease his father.

He tried to remember why, if they had all the privileges that everyone else dreamed about having, the two of them were letting adulting crush them into a fine powder before they were 30. The two were practically competing against each other for who had the most to prove.

Ben hung up with Melanie and spent the night on the couch of his office. After only about four hours he woke up stiff at the sound of his phone's alarm. He changed into a clean shirt he kept overnight and went back to the floor, ready to start the next day's shift.

Perhaps it was because he had no other aspirations, or because his trajectory was plainly laid out, but he didn't find the schedule all that grueling. It was 12 hours a day, every day, essentially. Sometimes more, sometimes not. Aside from a few sleep-deprived nights, the schedule kept him focused, usefully occupied, and under the watchful eye of his father and those that worked for him.

He certainly had no time to *spend* the money he was earning independently for the first time in his life. He was starting to invest it a little, now that he'd fully gotten over the learning curve.

He did have a little source of color in his life— no pun intended— and that was one of the young women who'd started work in the cafeteria two months ago.

He knew it was two months ago, because the kitchen started serving this brown butter chicken that nearly made him weep, and chicken fried steak with mashed potatoes, of all things. The associates fought sleep the entire day the first time it was served. The next time, two of them up and quit, one of them tearfully. The chicken fried steak was not served again.

A few weeks later she was out front on the line, serving. Ben couldn't stop staring at her. He was trying to figure out if she was indeed as beautiful as he thought she was. The sterile white cafeteria uniform and gratuitous chef's hats they all wore had a way of catfishing everyone.

It took him another week to speak to her.

Cynthia. Her name tag boasted her name. She was tall-ish and caramel-skinned with cool, translucent eyes. She didn't talk much, but of what she did say he'd detected an accent that he couldn't quite place.

"Are you the one responsible for the butter chicken?" he'd begun clumsily.

48

"Guilty," she'd replied, her tone cordial as she lazily blinked her gorgeous eyes and his heart nearly stopped. She gave him no smile.

He was bothering her.

It was an entirely foreign feeling. From women, at least. Ben had been overcompensating since he was a kid and entertaining unsuspecting nurses since he was a toddler. Besides, Ben had always been a good looking guy, always well-dressed, poised, always a Dvorak.

But here, he blended into a corporate, neo-con herd. He'd done so on purpose. And he was holding up the line.

He told her he wanted prime rib and she hastily picked up the big knife and serving fork.

"The chicken fried steak, too, I presume?"

She grinned as though flattered.

"My mother's recipe."

"We were all nodding off in front of our computer screens. Even Evan and he uses a stand-up desk," Ben nodded towards his colleague in line behind him.

She shook her head, smirking. She kept her composure long enough to lay his meat onto a steaming hot plate before she had to crack, thinking of some random associate falling asleep standing up like a horse.

"I was told it did not go over well," she said as she handed him back the plate heavy with prime rib.

"If it was your mother's recipe, I'm sure you know that's probably impossible."

She shrugged, carving roast chicken for Evan. "Not everyone likes perfection, I get it," she joked with a grin.

"Two of us quit the last time you served it," Ben said. She shook her head and rolled her eyes smiling as if refusing to be

49

blamed for that.

"It's true, it literally made them re-evaluate their entire lives," Evan filled in.

She gave Evan a laugh and Ben was instantly flooded with jealousy. He could feel Evan consequently growing in confidence, over a jar that Ben had loosened. Ben fought an eye-roll of his own.

He tried getting a little more small talk out of her every day, but unfortunately for him, she was a consummate professional. After two months, however, they'd managed a rapport of sorts. And she was used to seeing him as one of her first customers early in the morning.

This morning, Ben approached the company chow line with the usual spring in his step.

"Whatever's in that coffee pot, Cynthia, I need you to add rocket fuel to it."

"Another all-nighter?"

"I'm in the same pants I was in yesterday, Cynthia."

"I hadn't noticed," she managed a smile as she poured. "Anything else?"

"Nope. Gonna use caffeine and hunger to keep myself awake today."

"You're gonna keel over one day. 'Least if you were a doctor you could be saving lives," she shook her head.

"That may be the first time I've ever heard an opinion of yours."

"Oh yeah? How'd you like it?" she grins.

"...It's... not surprising."

"As in, stupid."

"Not in the least. At least it isn't anti-capitalist."

"Probably wouldn't go over well in a place like this, huh?"

"Not to mention completely contradict what you're doing right now, which is working for money."

"So it *is* a dumb one," she smiles.

"No."

"Liar."

"You're saying my time is better spent on a more tangible result, if I'm going to spend it to death."

Cynthia, nods her head this way and that, convinced that he wasn't just humoring her.

"Okay."

"It's not a stupid opinion. And not one I hear very often. Not to my face, at least."

"Can I ask you a question?" she suddenly said.

His body warmed, his insides flooded with excitement. Cynthia wanted to know something about him.

"Shoot," he answered.

"Sometimes I see you walking around on crutches..."

Oh. That.

It's silly that he almost forgets. Sillier that he expects everyone else to.

"Oh. Well, I was born with cerebral palsy. Six surgeries, physical therapy every day for twelve years, speech therapy, best specialists around the world, yadda yadda. Sometimes I have flare-ups, hence the crutches. Otherwise, I get around pretty good."

"I'd say you do. You're a lucky guy."

"Not lucky, just rich."

She had no idea who he was and who he was related to. How could she? She was basically the lunch lady. More beautiful than any lunch lady he'd ever seen, but still.

Cynthia shrugged, "A lucky sperm then," she unexpectedly

replied.

"Fair enough," he chuckled.

He paid her for the coffee, about to offer a cordial comeback. But after her comment, he couldn't help himself.

"What about you?"

"What about me?"

"You could be out in the world, saving lives with that beautiful face of yours, but instead you're here feeding rich white undergrads."

She laughed as she put his money in the till.

"Everyone's gotta eat."

"Not us," he scoffed.

"Even you," she insisted, her eyes a bit of a different color today, like a calico cat.

"That uniform is a crime against humanity, you know that?" he said, sounding offended.

She smiled. Big. As if she knew better than him what his compliment meant.

She kept her eyes on his hand as she playfully handed him back his change, coin by coin, careful not to touch him.

"My 'beautiful face' can save no lives. Trust me, I know," she mysteriously replied as she shut the cash register with her hip.

Time had utterly stopped once Cynthia opened her mouth to say a few more words to him than usual. The line was starting to bottleneck.

"Have a good one, Cynthia," he said, taking his time to put his change back into his pocket.

"Don't make me have to bring you a plate tonight, Ben," she shouted after him.

5

Present Day

Indigo Properties and Design is located in Tribeca— a modest-looking office space from the outside, but on the inside is modern and oddly homey, yet it makes the most of the building's industrial features at the same time.

Cynthia's now-signature sense of panache is practically everywhere. Splashes of color, unapologetic comforts, and sophistication are there to occupy the eye while waiting to see the guru herself.

Time seems to have suddenly sped up since he scheduled the meeting to finally lay eyes on Cynthia again. That is until he arrives. Now it seems like he's perpetually been waiting ten minutes. He absentmindedly adjusts the cuffs of his shirt sleeves protruding from his gray suit jacket.

The ten minutes drag on until the big doors at the end of the hall open. A pregnant woman emerges, followed by a casually dressed man with a murse and a long knitted beanie. One or both of them he recognizes as celebrities, but he can't quite place them in their plain clothes.

The guru emerges from her office closing the door behind her, to walk them out into the lobby. She pretends not to notice Ben sitting in the waiting area as she passes.

She's stylish and sharp, wearing an asymmetrical ribbed khaki-colored sweater and matching skirt, intimidatingly high neutral pumps on her feet. Her hair is long, unparted, and combed back like a waterfall, and he realizes it's the first time he's seeing her natural chestnut hair without any bold color enhancing. Shamelessly he watches her walk by in her expensive garb, relatively unrecognizable from the young, casual girl he fell in love with.

Ben's dating pool has stayed frozen in time since the last time he saw her: young, impressionable ingenues in their early 20's. But Cynthia is Cynthia. Youth is no replacement for Cynthia's allure, which cannot be manufactured and remains enticing at whatever age she is.

She is still very beautiful. She has a honed sophistication that he sometimes sees in professional women who are chronically successful and unmarried. But unlike most of those women, her air is warm, confident, approachable, like the girl he remembered.

Her Caribbean sea-colored eyes sparkle like gems and her red lips pop. No ring of any sort on her hands, which causes the tension in his shoulders to unconsciously release. He wrenches his eyes from Cynthia and catches her receptionist at the front desk looking away, head lowered and hiding a smirk.

Once her previous clients are gone, there is no more reason to ignore him. She takes a deep breath and makes a casual turn toward the sitting area. She gives him a comforting glance, the reassurance of her undivided attention.

"Mr. Dvorak," she can't help the fondness in her otherwise professional tone.

"Miss Gordon."

"You're early," she comments with a grin. He flashes a cordial grin of his own.

"Hardly. It's been far too long," he says as he stands and accepts her outstretched hand. She gives it a cute little shake and a smile emerges on her face. His heart flip-flops as they touch each other for the first time in ten years.

She is just as intimidating as she's always been to him. If he's matured at all in the last ten years, her peacock-colored eyes have dwarfed it. She has an age to her face only slightly beyond her years. Is he the cause? The notion makes him sick.

"Follow me. Jeanine, hold all my calls," Cynthia casually requests over her shoulder.

"Of course," Jeanine replies.

For a moment he thinks perhaps he is in the clear. That things are going to be as they were before any of the awfulness.

Then he remembers that he had to buy a property right out from under her just to get this meeting.

She leads him to an office space at the end of the hall that's mostly glass and overlooks the grounds in a small courtyard, a green rarity in the city previously part of an alley. Not as flashy as a corner office on the top floor of the Dvorak building, but impressive nonetheless.

She closes the door behind them and they are engulfed in uncomfortable silence.

Finally, they share the same space after a decade. He is every bit as handsome as he was then, she thinks.

Time has chiseled his jaw even further. His mother's Spanish dark eyes soften his sharp cheekbones and thick eyebrows. His face is more weathered than when he was 24, his features gaunt as if he's gone through something terrible and survived.

His scissored gait is nothing more than a conspicuous limp, the usual pendulum sway of his hips only slightly exaggerated. He must've had the surgery.

The innocence has been completely stripped from his eyes and she finds herself with a need to know his whole story. She folds her arms with a sigh.

"Okay. You're here to talk, so... talk," she says.

He huffs a little laugh. His inner optimist loses yet another bet, but a warmth fills his stomach. At least she isn't still smiling a syrupy smile of forgetfulness. Although he's not quite sure what she has to be so angry about.

"So that's how it's going to be?" Ben asks with a nod.

"You clearly wanted it this way, muscling me out like that."

"You forced my hand, Cynthia."

"And those are your first words to me in ten years?"

She's right, of course. The first words after ten years should be... so many other things. Namely, *Are you really a con artist? What did my father say to you? How can I fix this?*

"You're angry with me," he says.

"No."

"No?"

"It's business, I get it," she nods. "The permits were becoming a nightmare anyway. It's a beautiful house."

He means the past, but it seems to not be open for discussion. Not yet.

"I'll need someone to remodel it."

"You will."

"I trust you know the plans well enough."

"I do. And whoever you get to design it has a challenge on their hands."

"Cynthia..."

"You could try just saying what you want, instead of forcing us to share the same space."

Was any of it real? Why else would you be like this? Were you really just using me to get back at the company? What did he tell you? Why'd you take the money? Why would you trust his words over mine? Why? Why? Why? What are you doing later? The rest of your life? Have you found anything that tops what we had?

"I can't," he says instead.

"Why not?"

Because there's ten years of bad information between us, and it seems like you hate me now, even though I don't hate you at all.

"I received your check."

"I noticed. It was meant for your father."

"He didn't receive it. In fact, he doesn't receive any correspondence because he has Alzheimer's."

Cynthia does her best to hide her genuine shock. And what Ben could swear is concern.

"How long?"

"Not long. Less than a year, but it's a bit more aggressive than we anticipated."

"I didn't know."

"No one knows. We're not quite ready to announce it. I've been running the business side of things. Val handles the rest."

"I see."

A silence bobbles between them before he begins again. "I was sorry to hear about your mother. She was a cool lady. You have my condolences."

"Thank you," she says, quickly. Without flinching or emotion.

It's no surprise to him that her mother is a carefully guarded topic, now that she's gone. The two were closer than any mother and daughter he had ever seen.

"It's good to see you," he confesses.

"Is it?"

"Of course. My Junior VP raves about how happy his wife is with their remodel."

"And I'm sure you couldn't wait to drone on about how I used to pour gravy on your mashed potatoes. And how you banged me once."

"Once?" he asks.

He eyes her provocatively. Her body responds immediately, reminding her how long it's been. With anyone, but particularly this one, whose chemistry she's yet to match.

The thought leaves her noticeably witless. She turns to face the window as she walks behind her desk.

"In your stories, I'm sure it was only once," she finally replies.

"I'm surprised we've managed to avoid each other as long as we have."

"It wasn't easy, but I was devoted to the task."

"Until now?" he questions her.

She shrugs, facing him. "I suppose, but it was a risk I was willing to take. Check had to be written," she says, drinking the sight of him in a bit more. "Obviously, it was never meant to get to you."

"No. I'm sure whatever private confidence you shared with my father was typically respected."

"What the hell is that supposed to mean?"

"Nothing. It's just a little disturbing that after all these years you'd rather reach out to my father instead of me."

"Returning blood money is hardly 'reaching out.' Besides, it didn't concern you."

"The hell it didn't," he curtly said, showing his agitation. "What were the terms? $100K to get out of my life and never come back, or else?"

"More or less. You seemed to bounce back quickly."

Did he detect a tinge of jealousy? Ben relinquishes a smile as he finally makes his way to a chair, as if he plans to be there awhile. He tries not to seem desperate as he asks. "You mentioned extortion."

"Yes."

"Plus interest."

"Correct," she says without elaboration.

"That day you were fired... that's when he offered you the deal?"

"Right again."

Ben shakes his head a little. She doesn't seem ashamed. Or remorseful. Which is confusing.

"...Why?"

"Why what?"

"Why would you take his money?"

"Because *fuck* you. That's why, Ben. Any other questions?" she dares him. She looks him square in the eyes as she answers.

"I guess not," he blinks.

Cynthia's arms remain folded in front of her as she maintains her icy stare. She wrestles with what to say next, the temptation to continue exhuming the bones of the past overwhelming her.

"Why didn't you tell *me* you were engaged? To Melanie?"

Oh yeah. Melanie. His eyes dull with a flash of guilt, the pang of old mistakes. What could he say?

"It wasn't important enough to mention. At the time."

"I see. Sounds like we don't understand each other the way that we thought," Cynthia sighs.

The observation leaves him feeling hopelessly bitter but he has to concede.

59

"Seems that way."

"I hope you didn't come here looking for an apology. Or an explanation," Cynthia warns.

"I didn't," he lies.

"Because you're not getting either. I hate what happened, but it happened. Don't think because of what I just told you that I regret my decision one bit, because I don't. Because now I'm here. I'm my own person now and I'll never have to make a deal like that again."

"If that's what you have to tell yourself."

"I don't have to tell myself a *damn* thing. I suppose now you're gonna tell me that you were in love with me? You were gonna break off your engagement for me?"

Oh God, all this resentment over *Melanie*? What nonsense had she been telling herself for ten years?? She was so ill-informed it made him exhausted.

"I *did* break that off."

"And I'm sure it took a lot out of you. Telling a woman that you didn't love the truth."

"As a matter of fact, it did," he remembered, feeling strange to even have to bring up that part of his life as though it were as relevant to him as it was to her.

"You think she gave a shit if I *loved* her? I ruined the *plan*. We had our whole lives mapped out, since freshman year. My dad lost business when we... people like me have our lives written out in advance, and it's very hard to go against it."

"Which is why people like you *also* fuck the help, so excuse me if I don't play my violin for you. Do you really think you can make me feel bad for looking out for myself?"

So cold. The old man wins again.

"No," says Ben.

60

At least he got that explanation he was after. Though she didn't mean to give it. If his father could turn Melanie into a decade-old albatross for her, then it's likely his version of her is also some funhouse mirror exaggeration.

"Your father looked out for me more than you did."

"No argument there," Ben retorts somewhat bitterly. His mouth becomes a thin line as he twirls her business card absent-mindedly in his hand.

Either she couldn't, or didn't want to see that his father's money was still getting him what he wanted after all these years, which was to see the two of them apart. Even though she'd paid it all back. With interest.

"He gave me a story about you too, by the way. A completely different story."

At that, she stops. Her eyes narrow. She seems genuinely surprised, poor thing.

"What did he say?"

"So you *do* care what I think about you."

"I didn't say that."

"But you're curious?"

"I certainly believe that he lied to you about me. It's the only thing that would explain..."

She stops herself. This is exactly what she was afraid of. Him coming back around and bringing up unchangeable memories.

Now he is doing worse. He is messing with her mind.

"Look. Mr. Dvorak. There's a small part of me that feels... *endlessly* guilty. Endlessly. But it's *my* guilt, and I am very protective of it. I won't have you coming up here, judging me, understand?"

"Completely," Ben replies, switching gears at the sound of his formal title. "Forgive me, we're off-topic here. I know

61

you're a busy woman. As I was saying, I've recently acquired a property—"

"No, Ben."

"Why not?"

"I just... we can't work together. But it was good to see you and all. Really. It was foolish to avoid you this long. Honestly, I'm embarrassed about the whole thing."

"I understand. You must've been... afraid."

"Yes. No. I don't know, I don't think your father cared much after year six."

"Oh, believe me. He would've loved for you to make a wrong move."

"Don't be so sure about that, Ben."

Ben has no idea what Cynthia can mean by that, or how she could have more insight than he does on his own father. It's so perplexing, in fact, that he lets it go without another thought.

"Tell you what, I will let you sleep on this... business decision. A half-million-dollar inconvenience fee plus another unknown amount for a bathroom or two was a bit steep, as you can imagine. It only made sense to pay half that for a rundown house you already had time set aside to work on."

"You overpaid. By a hundred thousand dollars."

"I know," Ben remarks. "Compared to this shitty house, you're a bargain."

Cynthia goes rigid, her chest noticeably rising and falling rapidly.

"You bastard."

He shrugs. "Maybe I am. But you sort of walked into it."

Cynthia breathes, letting the remark roll off her back.

"Fine. Consider us even then, Ben. But one of those is all you get. Understand?"

62

"Fair enough. Anyway, I was happy to overpay. It got me what I wanted."

"Which was?"

"This meeting."

Cynthia successfully fights off a smile as she shoots him a look.

"Think about it. Get back to me. Maybe we'll have more time to reminisce."

Cynthia makes her way around her desk to wordlessly usher him out, but he ignores her cue, remaining seated.

"Oh, and I took the liberty of tracking down your partner. Gabriel? Nice guy."

She stops in her tracks. Son of a bitch.

"I told him Indigo Properties could name their price, and if hired would be given an unlimited budget. He seemed very excited."

There's no way she's going to be able to talk Gabe down from the ledge he would jump from if Ben really has gotten to him first. Suicide or none, she would have to find herself another business partner.

"I don't understand, Ben. I'm being as civil as I know how. You know I'm just going to be a bitch now."

"I'm sure you can manage to maintain the professional demeanor your clients have come to expect."

"Why are you forcing me to do this?"

Ben gave a shrug as he stood up, slowly and with obvious pain. He buttoned his coat.

"Like father like son, I suppose," he said over his shoulder as he let himself out.

* * *

63

"Jeanine, kindly see Mr. Dvorak out," Cynthia says over her office intercom once she makes it back to her desk.

"Of course, Miss Gordon."

"What else do I have today?"

"Nothing else until three."

"Cancel it."

"Yes ma'am."

Cynthia's professional exterior gradually begins to crumble after Ben's dramatic exit.

She reaches into her desk drawer and pulls out an expensive bottle of Glenlivet, the small glass tumbler wobbly in her shaking hand.

Emotion starts to well up, pining at the door of her soul like a stray cat, begging to be let in.

She opens the door and welcomes a brief deluge of sobs at her desk as ten years' worth of tension is finally released.

She wishes she had cigarettes. And also smoked.

He had an appointment, and she still wasn't ready.

The moment she closed the door behind them, a peculiarly strong urge came over her to instantly grab him by his lapel and let nature have its way. Peculiarly strong for being a decade old.

They had to do a lot of sneaking back then. They became adept at sensing when the coast was clear, when a room had thick enough walls, only one entrance. A corner office like this was a perfect place to hike up her skirt and get her rocks off with Benjamin. And one hell of a reunion.

But that was an obscenely dangerous can of worms. The reason why she still had to stay out of his way all these years. But the look in his eye was anything but nostalgic, and that was almost worse.

Damn these Dvoraks, Cynthia thinks, taking another sip. Sling-

64

ing their money around and sending their unwitting victims into emotional turmoil.

She reflects on her same crumbling composure that fateful day she was fired, the six-figure check growing damp in the grasp of her tight fist on the train. She didn't want to think about the implications of what she had done. She didn't want to think about leaving Ben behind like that, about whether or not Ben would make it without her when he told her time and again that he couldn't.

She only wanted to see the look on her mother's face as she told her that for the first time since Dad died, since the day they up and lost everything, that it was all about to *fucking* be okay.

6

Present Day

Two nights later, Cynthia lays in bed, staring at her phone with Ben's number in it, preparing to hit the Call button. She sighs.

She's already told Gabe that she'd accepted the job when she hadn't yet. She couldn't look into his excited, number-crunching face and tell him anything else. Any day he would be expecting an update. She could always put it off until tomorrow...

It's inevitable that she will have to get used to this, so she may as well get it over with. If she waits any longer, Ben will follow up first and blow her flimsy cover.

Cynthia presses the green button. On the second ring, she relaxes a little, realizing all prominent men are in bed by 9:30, and rarely answer their own calls. Especially from unknown numbers.

"Benjamin Dvorak."

Shit.

"Ben," she accidentally says, instead of his professional title. She gives her head a smack. Hoping he ignores it and keeps them off familiar terms. He doesn't.

"Cynth," he says.

She hears the smile in his voice as the nickname washes over her for the first time in ten years.

"You answer your phone this late?"

"I do, lucky for me."

Cynthia doesn't breathe. She makes an exaggerated series of facial expressions while plowing through her rehearsed pitch.

"So, Mr. Dvorak, I spoke to Gabe, and... even though we were adamant about not accepting any new business he's agreed to make an exception, considering your generous offer. It looks Indigo Properties has a new client."

"Wonderful."

"Great..." Cynthia replies awkwardly. Her mind blanks. Thankfully, Ben fills the silence.

"So, Miss Gordon. Now that I'm your client, what happens next?"

"Next, we walk the property, I tell you my vision, you tell me what you like and what you don't, I'll make rudimentary sketches throughout the process, show you my design choices—"

"There's no need to involve me that much. Like I said, Miss Gordon. I trust your instincts."

"The process will go much smoother if you participate in it, Mr. Dvorak. You only think you don't care about fixtures. Wait until I order the 'wrong' ones."

"Fine. As long as it entails seeing you, and I can fit it in my schedule, I'll meet you wherever you want. And call me Ben."

Maybe it was vigilance, or just long unfulfilled horniness, but everything he said to her sounded like sex.

"Right now the timeline is eight weeks, but that's, of course, if everything goes smoothly."

"Of course. And there's no need to rush."

"It would be better for you to get this done and back on the market sooner than later."

"You assume I will be selling it."

"Aren't you?"

"...I don't know," Ben admitted.

"Well, your decision will affect my design decisions. Whether I'm tailoring this for a buyer or for your own personal taste."

"Either way, I trust your judgment."

He was toying with her. He didn't care about this property. At all.

"Mr. Dvorak..." she sighed.

"Cynthia. You're calling me at home and it's after 9 pm. I wasn't being coy when I said to call me Ben. If you call me Mr. Dvorak again, I'll have to insist you tell me where you are so that we can have sex."

What... the *fuck*. Well, at least she knew it wasn't just horniness.

"I'll... keep that in mind. Ben," she stoically replies. "It's Miss Gordon to you, by the way," she adds, keeping it light.

Ben only laughs. "I really like that."

"You used to hate it back then too. When I called you that," Cynthia dares to reminisce.

"Because the only 'Mr. Dvorak' was my father, at the time."

"Grew into the title, did you?"

"Would you like to find out?"

Yes. Yes, she would. Arousal floods her body, turned on by his unexpected boldness, but also stunned. Everyone knows Esmee Ngozi is his fiancée.

She could give him a stern reprimand, but... he'll see right through her. That he's affecting her. And she needs to keep that under wraps until she can figure out what the hell his deal is.

"Aren't you engaged? Perpetually?"

"I am. How did you know?"

"You're not exactly a private figure," Cynthia insisted, down-playing her internet stalking.

"Anyway, she's not here," he conspicuously informs her.

Ew. If he's joking, it's falling flat. He can't seriously think she would want to entertain the idea of being his side piece. Again.

"Where is she?"

"Havana."

"Cuba?"

"The very one."

"Tell me about her."

"Really?" he skeptically asks.

"Sure."

"Well... she's a model. Her mother's English, her father's Nigerian."

"You sound like her Wikipedia page."

"It feels a little too weird talking to you about her, for some reason."

"Maybe because you know she wouldn't take too kindly to this conversation?"

"Are you kidding? She's a big fan. She practically begged me for an introduction."

"Don't think she has the same one in mind that you do."

"You'd be surprised."

Cynthia shifts uncomfortably in bed as he brags about all the action he's used to getting. Maybe she doesn't know this guy anymore.

"Okay... Mr.... Ben. We've strayed far off professional territory in a matter of minutes."

69

"You've lost your sense of humor over the years, I see. You started it, by the way. Miss Gordon."

"Hardly. Perhaps we should limit our correspondence to daylight. And only in person."

"You figure we're safer in person?"

Yikes. What does one say to that?

"The phone emboldens you, I think," she tactfully answers.

"Did you miss me?"

"Case in point."

"It seems like you did. I missed you. You look great. I meant to tell you."

She softens against her will. Two days ago it seemed impossible that their relationship could ever return to normal.

"You too," she smiles. "You got the surgery."

"I did."

"At whose recommendation?"

"My own."

"You said anyone who can't accept you the way you are can take a long walk off a short pier."

"Well. I changed my mind," he flippantly says. "I can have shower sex now."

"Oh," Cynthia laughs in nervous surprise. "Well. I suppose that's worth going under the knife."

"Remember how we used to shower together?"

"...Vaguely," she admits with a sigh, trying not to encourage him.

"I always found it weird that we never really tried to arouse each other, not on purpose, anyway. Just... made sure the other was clean, you know? Honestly, I thought it was out of guilt. But then, I kinda liked it. I started looking forward to it. Like a ritual. Every other woman I've tried it with couldn't wait to turn it into

70

sex. It's just not the same."

"...Where is this going, Ben?"

"Nowhere, apparently. What are you wearing?"

"...Ben."

"Miss Gordon."

He smiles, feeling like his old self again, not sure where or how he'd lost him.

Even over the phone, the sound of Cynthia's disapproval was enough to arouse him. If he's sensible, he should be worried about how reckless she's making him already. But he's tired of being sensible.

"What are you doing?" she mutters, mimicking the sound of his own inner voice.

"Making you uncomfortable. I don't remember it being this easy. Or fun."

"Well, it's not fun for me. None of this is. I take my work very seriously, and if I knew paying him back would lead to this, I would've kept the damn money."

Ben's pride takes a hit. It's been ages since he's had to work this hard. He soldiers on.

"You didn't answer my question. Miss Gordon. Surely you can afford lace these days," he prompts her again.

He's met with another sigh, and for a moment he thinks he'll get lucky and get her to cave. He stops breathing.

"I'm getting a bizarre feeling of deja vu," she reprimands.

"How so?"

"Oh, I don't know. Fiancées that I've never met, and your naive assurances that they would like me. And then you... doing this. And then my life blows up."

"That was a different situation."

"You, talking to me the way you should be talking to them.

71

You were bad news from the start."

"Don't say that. It's hurtful."

"You can't have me, and so you want me. Just admit it"

"That's not true."

"Isn't it? I don't remember getting any phone calls from you between fiancées."

"I meant the part where you said I can't have you."

Cynthia is silent for a while and he's never felt so shitty about being right. He wishes she would just tell him where she was right now. So he could go there. But that would hurt her.

"Anyway, I was avoiding you out of prudence, not fear," he defends. "He told us different things, you know. For all I knew, you were using me. To extort the company."

"....That's story your father came up with?" Cynthia gives him a shocked giggle.

"Essentially. Get close to the gimp, keep him happy. Blow his mind."

Cynthia laughs heartily at the premise— a poor consolation prize for ten lost years, he thinks, but somehow the most fitting.

She makes him feel like even more of an idiot for ever entertaining a picture of Dad's words coming out of Cynthia's mouth. But he can't help smiling.

"Just which part of that do you find funny?"

"Are you about to tell me that you actually believed that?"

"Not at first, but your actions didn't help. You disappeared. And then when you reappeared, you avoided me at every turn."

"Look, either we discuss the past, or I work for you. We can't do both."

"It seems you don't have much of a choice."

"Speak for yourself. I *always* have a choice, Ben."

"How is it that my father can force you to do things, but I

can't?"

Jesus, is he stuck up the past's *ass*. She can't do this. How was she going to survive the next eight weeks? Or more? His father was right. Ben was spoiled.

"Your father didn't force me to do anything, he was a strategist. And he didn't wear his heart on his sleeve like you, Benjamin."

"I'm just as shrewd as he ever was, Miss Gordon. You don't know everything about me."

"I don't have to. I've seen enough."

Ben stops. It's obviously too early to try and be anything more than civil. There are ten years of unspoken... whatever between them. Definitely too early to be flirting. And also, not appropriate.

But he's not sorry. After all this time, he can't help but feel entitled to it.

"So what? We're supposed to just... pretend as if none of it happened?"

"I'm calling you in a professional capacity, Ben. If and when I want to talk about the past, you'll be the first to know."

"Fair enough. In that case, it's late, Miss Gordon. If there's nothing else."

"Of course," Cynthia slowly rolls her eyes in defeat, replaying her behavior over in her mind. *Some professional*, she thinks.

"We'll discuss this tomorrow. My office knows my schedule. Find a time that works for you."

"Very well. I'll be in touch with your assistant, Mr... Ben. We should walk the property as soon as possible."

Ay yay yay, Cynthia blows a breath out of her cheeks once the phone call is over, her body tense, sweat forming in unseen places.

She's been bracing herself for how thoroughly he's moved on, and she doesn't know if tonight's phone call is proof that he has or that he hasn't.

Why should she recognize him at all? Ten years is a long time. And she basically ghosted him. Hard.

Was this descent into debauchery somehow her doing? She puts it out of her mind for the time being. How he makes her feel is of no consequence.

It's just another job, she thinks to herself. And that's how it's going to stay, even if it kills her.

* * *

The day he's to walk the property, Ben is rehearsing his apology in the twenty-minute cab ride across the bridge into New Jersey.

It only takes about twenty-four hours to perceive his behavior with Cynthia over the phone as cringe. He can barely re-live it more than a few seconds at a time, knowing that the next time they see each other he's going to have to address it.

He honestly hadn't thought any farther than the meeting, doing his best to show her that he was not the same spineless, naive boy she was probably only with out of pity, since he constantly insisted on those being the terms.

He's a man now, and not so afraid to lose, having lost her in the nightmarish way that he did. But since he got in that room with her, and it all came back with a vengeance.

Ben pulls up to a dilapidated house on Moss Lane, his brand new home. It looks like a 19th-century nightmare. The wood is rotting, the windows are broken. The gutters are full of birds' nests. It's an ugly green color with white trim and if that isn't bad enough, it shows signs of actually having been lived in. For a long time. He can see by the light of the cracked kitchen window a towering stack of what looks to be newspapers or magazines. It is a strangely large monstrosity on an even strangely smaller lot.

When his cab drives off he has to hope he's in the right place. It certainly doesn't feel like it.

Cynthia arrives on the property pulling up in a mid-sized, non-luxury brand car and looking construction chic, as though ready to work. With a gray checkered flannel shirt, form-fitting jeans and work boots. Her hair is pulled back in a fine, lengthy ponytail.

"You're early. Again."

Ben squints in the house's direction. "I didn't know if I was in the right place."

"You are. This is it. Like it?"

Ben wrinkles his nose. "It's... pungent."

"The previous owners had a few pets. And they were old. It's been in the same family for 70 years. They made quadruple on the deal, thanks to you."

His brow wrinkled worriedly. "They didn't die in there, did they?"

"Let's find out. Ready?"

"As I'll ever be."

Cynthia gives him a once over. "You're not exactly dressed to walk a property."

Ben looks down at his standard-issue dress shirt and navy slacks.

"I didn't think we were going to a haunted farm."

"Well... you are in Jersey," Cynthia jokes as they make their way up the walk.

The tall yellowish grass growing in between the cobblestone

pavement crunches underneath their feet. "You're right when you said I overpaid. What a paltry piece of land."

"Looks can be deceiving. There's a reason I offered what I did."

They go inside the creaking structure— creaking floors, intimidating architectural features with board and batten everywhere.

"I feel like an old-timey butcher standing in here."

"It's *beautiful*, isn't it? Practically everything on the house is original." Cynthia beams with her back to him as she looks around, dreamy-eyed. Finally, it's all hers to re-imagine.

Ben wasn't seeing the vision. "It's a museum. The city's going to give you a hard time."

"It's just outside the historical district. But I wouldn't care if they did, I'm not touching a thing. Nothing except the kitchen. Follow me."

They walked through the living and dining rooms to a room that was a narrow rectangle, as if standing on its head.

"This kitchen defies logic."

"I think it may have been converted. Several times."

"Is that a butler's pantry?"

"You know your stuff," Cynthia compliments him.

"I may have spent some time in an expensive house or two upstate," Ben chuckles.

When they get to the backyard he is greeted with a leafy expanse that seems to go on endlessly. The yard of each neighbor is plainly visible and does the same.

"See that? Half an *acre*."

"How are you able to find all this green in the city?"

"You just gotta know where to look."

Cynthia slowly walks a few paces ahead, and he shamelessly eyes the shape of her legs, her waist. Her bottom, in those jeans.

76

She hardly notices. Her girly shape is still there, but a little more... fluffiness.

He gulps. He's never been with a woman over 29. His mind gets caught up, thinking of a way he could somehow sleep with her with the jeans still on.

Meanwhile, Cynthia is looking at the ground, and yet she isn't. She is seeing something else. Something that will be there that is not yet there. She stops at around ten feet, drawing a line with her foot.

"There'll be an outdoor space here. And another. Outside the basement, that's going to be another living area. Maybe a second master."

"Sounds like you have big plans for this place."

"I do. I did. Honestly, this whole unlimited budget situation is messing with my mind."

"I could limit it. If you think that would help you."

"No, don't. It's a new challenge. A unique one."

"Listen, Cynthia..." Ben shakily begins, "I thought about it, and I've been meaning to apologize. About my behavior over the phone the other night."

"Don't mention it."

"It was... unprofessional, to put it mildly. Reckless. You could probably have me plastered all over the tabloids for what I said to you."

"I would never do that. We've got history. It's understand-able."

"Well, I want you to know, from here on out, I'll be 100% professional. It took me a minute to adjust. To seeing you again."

Cynthia's heartbeat was racing as she asked, "You're all adjusted now?"

77

"Honestly, no. But that shouldn't be your problem."

This is gonna be a looong eight weeks, Cynthia thinks. But she's relieved, somehow, to know that it was going to be tough for him too.

Should she make it tougher?

Yes. Yes, she should. Only one of them has a fiancée. Serves him right.

Cynthia shrugs, "As I said, don't mention it, Mr. Dvorak. Besides, I appreciated the fap material."

Ben raises an eyebrow, not quite believing his ears.

"What?"

"Hm?" Cynthia responds. A grin blooms on her face.

Ben is now locked behind his 100% professional promise. He still wears a stunned look on his face as he glares at her with resentment, as if she's taken the only life raft off a deserted island. Cynthia laughs, finding his misery amusing. It's probably wrong how much better it makes her feel.

"See? My sense of humor is still intact. Let me show you the upstairs," Cynthia says while Ben is still speechless.

Cynthia leads him back inside to a narrow staircase that leads to a spacious second floor with three bedrooms, a bathroom, and a parlor space separating them. She bounds up the first few stairs before she turns around, waiting for Ben who's still on stair number two.

"Sorry, I know this is probably killing your legs."

"No big deal. I'll get there."

"I could have a service elevator, put in, y'know. There's already a little laundry chute back here."

"No need. That is, if I decide to sell."

"Well, that's something I need to know pretty soon, don't you think?"

The tour ends in the master bedroom which is very large with a criminally small window.

"I'm no designer, but I'm guessing you're going to make this window bigger."

"I'm gonna do more than that," Cynthia answers excitedly. "This window is going to be transformed into a balcony."

"How are you going to manage that?"

"It's surprisingly easy *and* cheap. Which usually fills me with special joy, but... with an unlimited budget, it does next to nothing."

"Welcome to my world," Ben scoffs.

"But it's still very cool and will sell this house in a heartbeat."

"I told you, I don't know if I'll be selling or not." His reply makes Cynthia relinquish an exasperated sigh.

"You obviously know what you're doing, your vision sounds great," he reassures her.

"'Sell it,' 'don't sell it'... Ben, if you're going to hire me, then I need a reason to do this project, a purpose."

She smells the same and he's trying to determine the source. Surely she's not using the same shampoo from ten years ago. Surely this isn't her naturally sweet smell.

Ben figures she probably wouldn't appreciate his entirely selfish reasons for buying this house. This meeting alone made it worth spending the money. Shooting the shit, getting to smell her. But in truth, he had no plan for the property, and they both knew it.

"Fine. I'm probably never going to live in Jersey for any reason, so let's sell it," he settles.

"Great. That's going to require a lot less of your time. I'll need your input on some things since you're still the client.

"I suppose. Maybe we can all have dinner?"

Cynthia cocks her head. "We?"

"Of course. Esmee would love to meet you."

"I thought she was in Havana?"

"She was. She's back now. Just for a few days. Our life is a series of... very long layovers."

"Sounds... exciting," Cynthia diplomatically responds. "Does she know that you tried to sleep with me in-between 'layovers'?"

"Again, I apologize for that. But if you consider that 'trying,' then you definitely need to get out more than you currently are. Starting with dinner."

"...That isn't some kind of weird freaky couples code for a threesome is it?"

Ben laughs.

"We don't bite, I promise. I didn't mean to spook you."

"You didn't spook me."

"That was a joke, okay? Anyway, I'm not a threesome guy. At *all*, you know that."

"I think I recall that conversation," Cynthia smiles. Ben finally tears his eyes away from her blushing cheeks.

"We'll coordinate schedules," he says before she can object. "I'm dying to catch up with you. Properly."

He doesn't seem to get that she'd rather eat nails than have dinner with him and his fiancée. The very thought of it is tanking her morale.

But she won't be able to avoid the girlfriend, it seems. She never could. It's just as well. Being alone together is a pile of bad news. Even in this busted up fixer that smells like cat piss, she can sense it.

Nevertheless, she musters up a professional, grinning face.

"Likewise," Cynthia answers stiffly. "I look forward to it."

7

Ten Years Ago

"Ban ya belly, gyal," Cynthia's mother Bev sighed into the darkness, "Ah got bad news."

"Oh no. On a scale of 1-10?"

"....8."

"Alright. Hit me."

Cynthia was so mature. It tore Bev up more than ever having to rely on her daughter now that everything's gone to shit, now that Winston was gone. Nearly a decade now.

"I didn't get deh job," Bev confessed.

"Yuh makin' joke!" Cynthia answered in an indignant patois. "They made you do all that paperwork and everything!"

"Dey went wit' someone else."

"I don't get it. Your degree was supposed to help. Who has more experience than you??"

"It's okay. It jus' means 'tings get delayed a little bit. If we find a place by October—"

"I'm really doing good at this job, mom."

"Ah know, ah know."

"I don't want to leave. You know the shelters around here are no good."

"Ah shoulda jus' had yuh go to school, enuh? Deh shelters fuh older women are decent, enuh. Yuh would at least have a warm place to stay. *Food,* enuh."

"School costs money. And I could give a shit about... *curriculum* right now. Senior year was stressful enough."

"Yuh too young to be worryin' about me, Cynti. We'll figure somet'ing out, I promise."

After a silent moment, Cynthia began with a sigh.

"...So, there's this boy. At work."

"Boy, wha boy?"

"Well... I guess he's more of a... man. A young man."

"Is dis 'young man' one a' da *stock brokers* ya boss warned you about, eh?"

"Virginia's not my boss, and I don't think he's a stockbroker, but yes. In fact, I don't know what he does."

"I see. He likes you?"

"Yes."

"And yuh like him back, awat?"

"I don't know, I don't know him very well. But he's gorgeous. He had cerebral palsy as a kid...or... I guess he still has it... he got 'dis likkle *limp.* Likkle *hop and drop* enuh," she smiles, glancing in her mom's direction. Bev gives her an enthusiastic laugh, already shipping this relationship by the sound of it.

"He has this look in his eyes, that's like a mix of kindness, compassion. Some kind of... pain. And then a little arrogance. A likkle *pomposity*, enuh. 'Cause he's rich? Just feels like I'm gonna *die* when he looks at me. Oh, and I'm pretty sure he's the son of the guy that owns the entire building."

"Oh, *gosh*. Well, did he ask yuh out?"

"Not yet, but he will."

"And yuh'fraid yuh might fire de wuk."

"Among other things."

Cynthia left it vague for the sake of her mom, who understood. Bev was grateful to have a daughter that wasn't itching to get into trouble and felt comfortable enough to tell her everything, even if it were on a slight delay. If Cynthia was concerned about a boy, then the boy had to be a pretty big damn deal.

"Well... jobs are everywhere, enuh. But a good guy is hard to find. Is he worth losin' yuh job over?"

"I don't know."

"Do yuh know anyt'ing, Dan?"

"Nothing. And I'm not sure, but I think he has a girlfriend."

Bev smiled. Cynthia's father Winston was engaged at the time they met. When they first made love it was like making love to the lightning. He sacrificed his entire reputation when he broke off the engagement. But he did it. She respected him for that. He could've gone through with it, could've kept Bev on the side. Lord knows she was smitten enough to have gone right along. But then, she wouldn't have had Cynthia.

"Well, yuh grown now, Cynt'ia, ent? A *smart* one, enuh. Focused. Yuh not easily fooled. Even as a baby, enuh. Yuh don't need my advice, not dat I have any t'give. Except... follow yuh heart."

Cynthia gave a long sigh that signaled to her mother that she would likely be up for a while. Thinking. Bev remembered the feeling. Like seeing a tidal wave from a distance and only gathering more momentum.

Love. Bev could only be there for her when it came. And hope that she didn't get capsized.

* * *

"Cynthia gave me an extra banana, guys," Dev said with two raised eyebrows of innuendo.

"We seriously need a day off. We're all fantasizing about the same chick like we're in a hippie commune," Evan said.

"Cynthia's a 10 in the real world. I've got evidence."

"What evidence?"

Dev pulled out his super-secret laptop and opened up MySpace, finding Cynthia's profile.

"You're friends with her on MySpace?"

"No, but her profile is public."

"Dude, you're disgusting," Ben shook his head.

"What? It gets boring around here. If I'm gonna look busy, I need to be looking at something interesting."

"Dev, you better not be jacking off to any of this."

"Relax, Ben, no one's beating off to your girlfriend," Evan rolled his eyes.

"Speak for yourself," Dev smirked.

"She's not my girlfriend, obviously."

"Sure. Because no one's ever had a fiancée and a girlfriend before."

"Oh shit, I found a swimsuit pic."

"I don't wanna see," Ben replied.

"Wanna be surprised?" Evan ribbed him.

Ben didn't like Evan's tone. Ever since he made her laugh for that one moment in history, he'd been acting like he actually had a chance with her— and didn't want it. Now he was further pretending like he wouldn't care if others had a chance.

"Dude, why are you still on MySpace anyways? Everyone's on Webster now."

"I'm leaving," Ben announced.

"Yeah right, we have a presentation due in two hours," Dev

furrowed his brow.

"Yeah, well, my brain's fuckin' fried and I need a cigarette," Ben said, making his way out the door.

"Dude, forget him. It's not like Ben can get fired anyway," Evan muttered under his breath.

"Yeah Evan, and I'm still running circles around you, how do you explain it?" Ben retorted on his way out, having heard his comment.

Evan just scoffed as Ben made his way outside, to the service entrance.

Ben lit his long menthol cigarette, extra annoyed, mostly at himself for letting Evan's comments get to him. Even now, he guessed that they were talking about the "over-privileged golden boy" while he was gone. "Crippled fuck," they were probably saying.

Ben took another long drag, shaking his head. Between his disabilities and his family, he was being underestimated all the time. He was either being told things would be impossible for him, or unfairly easy. It was maddening. He needed this two or three minutes of chit chat today with Cynthia like nobody's business.

It took a few weeks to catch on, but eventually Ben came to learn the routine of Cynthia's breaks.

He'd first caught her walking outside during his afternoon break nearly two months ago. It jarred him, to see Cynthia on her own time. He couldn't believe it the first time he saw her hair without that chef's hat. At the time, it was a dyed blonde color. He'd curiously watched her, to see what she would do.

He figured out she got two fifteen-minute breaks, but he couldn't figure out what she was doing with her 30-minute lunch.

Then one day he saw her being picked up by someone, either her mother or sister or... some relative. Carrying a bag full of takeout trays, presumably full of food.

So that's what she was doing with her lunches.

Surely they weren't charging her for taking extra food they were just going to throw away. He thought about asking about it, but it would only rock the boat in some unintended way. The way he got his favorite nanny fired by telling his mom that she sometimes took naps on the couch while he watched tv.

This day she was waiting out back near the dumpsters, likely waiting on her mystery driver. He sauntered over to her.

"So what's a smart girl like you doing working in a cafeteria? Shouldn't you be in college? Going to football games? Studying... whatever pretty girls study?"

She startled, turning around briefly as he sauntered up next to her.

"So you have no idea what pretty girls study, huh? Telling."

"Smooth, Cynthia. You can't avoid all my questions forever."

"I'm not avoiding them, I just find your questions more interesting than my answers."

"You've managed to fool me into thinking we've been having conversations for two months almost. If I didn't know any better, I'd think you were trying to avoid talking to me."

"But you do know better," she said. She smiled.

"I actually don't mind it. It's helping me work up my detective skills."

"Oh?"

"Like, the fact that you never take lunch and you always leave with bags of food. And then a lady that I assume is your mother picks you up every other weeknight on the dot."

"Uh-huh."

"And that it's September and you still work a full day, so you obviously aren't attending any kind of school. Which brings me back to my opening question," he said, obviously waiting for her to fill in the blanks.

Cynthia gives a sigh.

"My mom is... we fell on a bit of hard times. For awhile. And it's just me and my mom, so... the plan was just to take a year off, work to help us get back on our feet, and then on to culinary school. The plan's taking a little longer than we thought, but... it's still the plan."

"See, now was that so hard?" he smiled.

"It was a little hard," Cynthia suppressed a giggle.

"What do you do on the other days that she doesn't pick you up?"

"Take the train."

"The train, where?"

"Across the bridge."

"To Brooklyn?"

"Jersey."

"Ah. Jersey. That's where you live?"

"Yeah." Cynthia clenched her butt, hoping he would leave it at that.

"Well, if you ever need a recommendation, let me know."

"Thanks."

"I'll be starting school myself, soon. Graduate school, that is."

"MBA?"

"How'd you know?"

"Took a guess. Hear a lot of chatter about it in the cafeteria."

"Those guys aren't bothering you, are they?"

"No one bothers me, actually. Except for you."

87

"I can't help myself. It gets boring around here. You're too beautiful to be working in a cafeteria."

Cynthia gave him a luminous giggle that he relished.

"What's funny?"

"My boss said you would say that."

"Your boss?"

"He told me the same thing, and then he said 'you're going to hear it about a hundred times, so get used to the idea.'"

Ben smiled, the laugh lines around his eyes barely pronounced. "Your boss sounds like a decent guy."

"He is."

"You have an accent," he blurted.

"Do I?"

"Faint. Caribbean, I'm guessing."

"Very good. My mother's from Grenada."

"I'm going to... look that up tonight."

"You should," she chuckled.

"Anyway, let me know if you ever want to see Princeton. I could show you around."

"...I'm sure you could," Cynthia replied with a sly look in her eyes.

Ben's mouth went dry involuntarily. He lifted his hands in surrender.

"I'm just offering as a friend. Honestly. I have a... girlfriend, anyway."

"Really?" she answered flatly.

"Yeah. Don't sound so surprised, Cynthia."

"I'm not surprised..." Cynthia began, then stopped herself. Inwardly she was frantically trying to make herself disappear. "I don't think she would appreciate this conversation at all."

"Well that's where you're wrong," Ben volunteered, as if clueless to her meaning. "She'd love you. She's very philanthropic."

"Likes helping out the less fortunate, does she?"

"I didn't mean it like that."

"Listen, Ben. You should probably get back in there."

"Relax, hall monitor I will. Think about what I said, Cynthia. About Princeton. You should see what college is like before you nix it altogether."

"Don't really have money for Princeton."

"There you go again, shutting things down before they start. You gotta learn to think big, Cynthia. Then the resources come. Think about that."

She honestly couldn't tell if he was joking or not. His dad owned the fucking building. The hell was he even talking about?

"You really shouldn't smoke. It's bad for you," she answered back.

He gave her an even bigger heart-melting smile.

"Is that you giving me a taste of my own medicine?"

"Maybe."

He flicked his cigarette and headed back inside, his hands retreating to his pockets. "Later, Cynthia."

"Good talk, Ben."

Cynthia shook her head as Ben left her side, remembering Virginia's pep talk when she first got hired. *They're cute, they're young, and they'll try to flirt with you.*

"Be nice, but don't encourage them," she finished out loud. She was pretty sure she'd done that. Even though all she wanted to do is try her worst without using anything but her eyes.

She could try telling Ben to just go away. She didn't know him very well, but she knew he wouldn't take kindly to that. She didn't want to ever find out Ben was the type of guy Virginia warned them about. *It's not gonna end bad for them, it'll only end*

89

bad for you.

* * *

Cynthia requested more time in back of house after that conversation outside the service entrance. And Cynthia changed up her routines so that they barely caught each other's breaks.

On the night the associates got their bonuses several weeks later, however, the Dvorak Group held a banquet. The kitchen staff catered and all the associates were there, including Ben.

Cynthia's limbs had been quaking the whole night, she was so nervous to see him, and every time he stole a glance in her direction it sent shockwaves to her heart because it meant he'd caught her doing the same. Ben cornered Cynthia after everyone had been served.

"Are you stalking me, Cynthia?"

She smiled. "If it pays time and a half, then yes that's what I'm doing."

"Any progress with culinary school?"

Cynthia rolled her eyes as she shook her head.

"What?" he grinned.

"I should've never told you that."

"What, that you have dreams? You're right, I am the wrong person to tell."

"If it means that you're going to badger me about it every time you see me, then you *are* the wrong person."

He chuckled a bit and hung his head, as if nervous. "I just don't want you to wake up one morning and realize that it's been ten years, and you still work in the cafeteria of the Dvorak building. Is that so wrong?"

Cynthia didn't notice, playing devil's advocate. "You never

know, I could become head chef on my own, without having to go into debt."

"Not all debt is bad, you know. Sometimes it's necessary. And I hate that school is getting such a bad rap. School exists so that you won't be a moron. It would make me very sad to see you excel here."

"And why's that?"

"If I'm not one day getting postcards from you from exotic and faraway places, it would make me very sad."

"Or whatever we'll be sending each other in the future."

"There'll still be postcards in the future, Cynthia."

"Don't be so sure," she answered as though she knew something he didn't. He chuckled.

Across the room, Sol Dvorak noticed that his son seemed to be spending a lot of time chatting up the help.

"So... I have a school thing that would be perfect for you to go to. I want you to come."

"Are you joking?"

"Nope. Friday. You'll have to wear something nice."

Cynthia's eyes widened a moment.

"I... usually dye my hair on Friday nights."

"Cynthia, you're breaking my heart, here. You've known me for a long time."

"If serving you breakfast and lunch for four months is knowing you, then the answer is definitely no."

"It isn't. Aren't you curious about me at all?"

Cynthia had to laugh as she shook her head.

"Your dad has been watching you talk to me for quite some time, so I don't know how that would go over."

Ben stopped abruptly, with a wrinkled brow and a smile. "My dad? How do you know who my dad is?"

Cynthia chuckled as if he were adorable.

"I... figured it out."

"How?"

"Sorry, was it supposed to be a secret?"

"No, it's just... how long have you known?"

Cynthia didn't know how to answer. She seemed to agitate him.

"Awhile. I mean, I didn't know your last name at first, but I always suspected."

"Shit."

Virginia didn't mention that they were all clueless about themselves. Cynthia felt that should be remedied.

"Everyone told me not to bother you, that you were the owner's son."

"Who's everyone?" Ben's brow wrinkled further.

"I didn't mean to upset you."

"You didn't. I just... if you knew, you didn't let on. I'm impressed, I guess."

"If I agreed to go out with you, I'd find out anyway, right?"

"...Sure."

"It's okay not to pass for regular, you know," Cynthia reassured him.

"That's not what I was doing."

"Okay. But if it makes you feel any better, I probably would've figured it out."

"What would make me feel better is if you agree to go see Princeton with me."

"I'm afraid I don't have anything suitable for a night like that."

"Let me buy you something."

Oh no. "Ben..."

"I'm not taking no for an answer."

"Why?"

"Because I just became a junior associate and I need to see what's under that chef's hat."

Cynthia chuckled.

"You'd like it," she divulged.

"Really?" he asked in wonder.

She let another laugh escape as she nodded.

"Benjamin, you're missing the party," Joshua, one of his father's cronies came to fish him from the banquet table.

"I'm waiting for a new smoked trout platter," Ben fibbed.

"He's not bothering you, is he?" Joshua addressed Cynthia with a smile, his cordiality a very thin veneer.

"No, sir, he's just... being polite."

"Cynthia here is thinking about going to my alma mater. We were just having a conversation about that," Ben filled in, with a thin cordial veneer of his own.

"Cynthia?" the man inquired.

"That's what her name tag says," Ben conspicuously replied. "The same name tag she's worn every day for three months."

"Well, let Cynthia get back to her work so that she's not reprimanded by her boss."

"We wouldn't want that," Ben looked at Joshua, letting his agitation show.

For the first time, Cynthia saw Ben become the boss's son.

Oh boy.

She looked over at Virginia who quickly turned her head away from the scene, obviously having been looking at them.

"Sir, I can have a server bring you whatever you like once it's ready," Cynthia suggested quickly, her head down as she switched out platters.

Ben's jaw clenched. It seemed like every person in his life was there to remind him who he could and could not associate with, to uphold some invisible barrier that needed constant maintenance and surveillance. It irritated him.

They had to do that because it wasn't real. Everything real just *exists*, whether people liked it or not. And yet the people around him were eager to hold up illusions. Even his sister Valerie, who was as down to Earth as a Dvorak could get.

Even more, it irritated him that a smart girl like Cynthia knew how to comply. No doubt many people had convinced her that it was "smart" to do so. It was all a sick game of control.

"Sounds perfect, Cynthia," Joshua said with a severe stare aimed at Ben that Cynthia pretended not to notice.

Ben returned the stare until Joshua finally stood down, ultimately knowing his place. He walked away and Ben finally turned his attention back to Cynthia, who was acting very very busy.

"Listen, I don't know what I said to you the last time we talked, but it seems like you're acting weird, and I think it's whatever this place is doing to you."

Cynthia was sure her heart was going to pound itself right out into the open. Ben was agitated, and some of it was aimed towards her. He'd felt her absence. And he didn't like it.

"Next Friday night. You're coming with me."

"I need this job, Mr. Dvorak," she said.

"Don't do that. Not you too."

"Not me what?"

"You may be the only friend I have in this entire building. Don't take that away from me."

Cynthia sighed, looking over at the other side of the room, where she seemed to have caught the attention of the CEO. Ben seemed unfazed. She returned her attention to the large metal catering trays.

"I have no idea what to tell my mom," she made the excuse.

"Tell her the truth. That I'm taking you to see the Princeton campus."

"She's going to have to... meet you and all that."

"That's fine with me."

Cynthia rolled her eyes again.

"What, you never been on a date before?" he smiled.

Cynthia couldn't control her blush. It wasn't a date with an unavailable guy, it was worse than a date. It was something "friendly," without boundaries. And she couldn't deny she was into it.

A work-free day with Ben. Telling stupid jokes and trying to get her to open up. She wanted him to keep prying at her like a stubborn oyster. She wanted him to keep trying and failing. Dusting himself off undeterred and trying again.

"A date? Is that what this is?"

"No, but it's what all moms think this is."

"I was more of a 'sneak out of the house' kind of girl," she said. He laughed.

"When your mom comes to pick you up the night before, I'll come out and say hi, let her know the plan. The next day, we go. It's at 7, but we can go straight from here."

He conspicuously had it all planned out. Cynthia only felt— never saw— multiple sets of eyes on the two of them.

"If I say yes, will you get away from my station?" she asked.

"Yes."

"Then yes."

Cynthia didn't see Ben again that week at all, until her mother came and picked her up the evening before, just like they had planned.

Ben came limping his way out to the service entrance on his break. He loomed over the passenger window of Bev's van— also Bev and Cynthia's house, unbeknownst to him.

"Wah say, Cynthia's mom," Ben debuted his Grenadian slang. Cynthia gave her mom a funny look and cracked up. Bev eyed him with amusement, genuinely impressed.

"I'm good! Wah go, Shatta?" Bev sent back.

"Taking a trip?" he says when he sees the trunk area stacked with boxes and bedding.

"Some'ding like dat," Bev answered, with a much stronger accent compared to Cynthia.

"Cynthia tells me you're from Grenada."

"I am."

"How long since you've been back?"

"Oh my. Since Cynt'ya was about 10. For her faddah's funeral."

"I'm so sorry. My condolences."

"T'ank you, dear."

"I hope Cynthia explained to you what we're doing. I'll have her home by 10."

"Ah'll be pickin' her up," Bev insisted.

"Are you sure? It's a bit of a drive."

"It is, but not from where ah go t'school," Bev assured him.

"I could just stay with you," Cynthia piped up in Ben's direction. The corners of his mouth went down as he shrugged.

"If... that's okay with your mom, it's okay with me," Ben managed a response so diplomatic Bev wondered if Cynthia was barking up the wrong tree. Bev's eyes met her daughter's.

"He lives in the city, I can go straight to work. No subway fare."

Bev felt a little strange even being there. Cynthia was 21, an adult now in every way. If she was going to sleep with some boy, why did Bev need to know about it at all?

Either Cynthia genuinely didn't think this would lead to more sleepovers, or she was so afraid to tell her mother what a terrible job she was doing, that she was going to have to get a boyfriend just so she could sleep in a warm bed this winter.

"Call me when yuh make it back, enuh." Bev replied.

"I will," Cynthia agreed.

"Okay. T'morrah den?"

"Tomorrow. Bye, Mama."

"Nice to meet you, Ms. Gordon," Ben said, his world-class manners exceeding their own.

"Call me Bev," Bev smiled, instantly charmed.

He did call her Bev. Every other day when she came to pick Cynthia up. And she called him "Benji," the first person ever to give him a nickname. Soon, she stopped having to pick Cynthia up altogether. Because Cynthia was going to his place after her shift when he wasn't home. And when he usually just spent the few hours he had to sleep in his office, he instead rushed back to his place, where he would wake Cynthia, no matter what time of night it was, and they would sometimes talk. And eventually, make love.

The first time he woke to her face, her body in his bed, it startled him the way it made him feel. It was borderline guilt. Maybe he felt like he was cheating. Maybe he knew that he was. Even though he'd told Melanie about Cynthia. Even though he'd mentioned matter-of-factly that she was staying there sometimes, when they talked on the phone. He'd convinced himself that if he could talk about it openly that it was a sign that there was no danger.

97

But the day Cynthia asked if they would ever know what it was like to kiss, he knew he was a goner.

"One day we will," he'd answered. He couldn't say 'yes,' but he sure as hell couldn't say 'no.' His answer scared him. It meant he longed to be free to kiss her. He knew that already, but he didn't know he planned to make it a reality. Not until he knew that Cynthia might be feeling the same.

8

Present Day

When Cynthia arrives at the agreed-upon restaurant location, it is Esmee who greets her first, dressed in a little black dress. Cynthia deduces that she is at most a size zero. In the black dress, she practically disappears. Esmee greets her with a hug as though they've known each other well.

"I'm underdressed," Cynthia says when she sees Ben in a dress shirt and slacks. Cynthia dressed casually but elegantly in long loose khaki trousers and a sleeveless white shirt equally loose, a wife-beater but expensive looking. A turquoise pendant hung from her neck and hovered over her modest cleavage.

"Nonsense, you're our celebrity guest," Esmee insists. "I'm sure you're familiar with Benjamin's monotone wardrobe. Or was he more casual back then, when you were together?"

Ah. We're getting formalities out of the way, I see, Cynthia thinks.

"I seem to recall a t-shirt or two," Cynthia teases him.

"When Benjamin said the two of you used to fancy each other I couldn't believe it," Esmee marvels.

"How's our investment coming along?" Ben asks, ignoring

his wife-to-be.

"Dismally," Cynthia replies.

"Didn't Barrett handle the building codes problem?"

"It's not the city, it's me. I can't seem to get... inspired. Or maybe I'm too inspired. It's making me indecisive."

"Didn't you already have big plans?"

"I did. But then... I started changing things."

"The unlimited budget," Ben smiles.

"The unlimited budget."

"I can get rid of it."

"Please don't, it's glorious," Cynthia sighs.

Ben laughs. It doesn't take more than a few minutes for Esmee to feel left out.

"Tell me everything," Esmee says, putting a hand on hers. "How did you become the elusive 'Cynthia Gordon'?"

"I hardly know," Cynthia chuckles.

"You're notoriously guarded about your life in the press. Is it true you've only been at it five years?"

"Well... not exactly. My first project was technically my first house. This beat-up old rehab that my mother and I found. Dirt cheap. We bought it with cash..." Cynthia's voice tapers off.

She wants to shoot herself, talking about what she did with the check right in front of him. She can feel the bile rising up. Esmee reaches out to touch her hand again.

"I'm sorry. I know losing your mum was hard. I don't know what I'd do if I lost my mum, I'd go stark raving mad."

"It's... okay," Cynthia dismisses with a shake of her head. She doesn't dare look at Ben as she presses on.

"Um, so it took about three months to fix it up. It was just the two of us. I was afraid to hire anyone else out so... we did a lot of the labor. That we had no business doing," Cynthia gives a laughing roll of her eyes at the memory. "But I learned a lot that way. I figured out I had an eye."

"Someone just came by and offered to buy it straight away?"

"No. We lived in it for a few years. Then my mom passed and I couldn't bear to look at it anymore. But it hurt even more to sell it."

"Not for long. Selling a flip for pure profit. You must've made a pretty penny," Ben mutters. His tone sends icicles up and down her spine.

And now he knows. She just wishes he understood.

"Indeed," she admits.

"You turned right 'round and did the same thing again," Esmee infers.

"Yes. Only this time I hired a crew. Same crew I still use. Lived in that one and watched the prices in the neighborhood."

"And then the girl with one house bought two," Ben deduces.

"And so on and so on," Cynthia concludes, thrilled to be done with the story.

"Well, you're a genius. Everyone knows a Cynthia Gordon job when they see one. You did the white party in the Hamptons."

"Well, I just did the design and I left. For free, actually. I didn't want to, Gabe forced me to. He's always forcing me to see the big picture. I only knew the guest list after the fact. I heard it was a great party."

"Why didn't you come??" Esmee gasps, ignoring Ben's attendance being her possible impetus for skipping it. Luckily, the truth is much less exciting.

"I wasn't invited."

"You're joking!"

"I'm serious. I wasn't known for that sort of thing, so I think they were afraid for me, in case the design didn't go over well."

"Most people don't notice details like that, but I'm absolutely mad for ambiance. What makes people feel open and happy. A space can really affect a person's mood. It's fascinating to me. I'm thinking of going into it once I'm done with modeling."

"You should," Cynthia encourages her.

"I still have a decent window to keep doing what I'm doing. I know I could make a name for myself. A brand. Benjamin's agreed to help me," she says, her hand going to his knee in a loving gesture.

"He does love to help the ladies," Cynthia found herself saying. Oh geez. She needs to get out of here.

"How do you mean?"

"I... don't know," Cynthia shrugs with a plastic smile.

"How did you get into this line of work anyway?" Ben suddenly blurts, as if unconvinced.

"Were you even listening just now?"

"Not really," he lies.

"It's not a 'line of work,' it's a passion. I chose it, it wasn't handed to me."

"Because my company was *handed* to me?" Ben fills in. She shrugs.

"If the shoe fits," Cynthia mutters.

"Let's not pretend you're immune to unfair advantages, Cynth," Ben alludes.

Cynthia stares at him, trying to maintain decorum. Her pride singed as Esmee eyes the two of them.

This is madness. She has another discouraging flash of hopelessness. Swinging from insults to flirts to the decrepit sidewalks of memory lane. This. Wasn't. Going. To. Work.

"I'm going to punch you in the fucking face. Is that what you want?" Cynthia says to Esmee's surprise. She giggles with delight. They really did have a relationship.

"You're very well dressed and I think I'd like to see that," Ben confesses.

"You're the one pretending, by the way. Not me," Cynthia cryptically digs before taking a drink of her cocktail.

"You haven't answered my question."

"Which was?"

"This line of— this 'passion' of yours. When I met you it was food," Ben asserts, accusatory.

"It still is food. And also this."

"You realized you'd much rather be the one eating?"

"No. I was 20 years old then, I'm allowed to change my mind. Besides, one summer in your kitchen, and I was cured," Cynthia defensively clarifies.

Ben frowns. "What's wrong with our kitchens?"

"Nothing. It was actually a great experience. I gave it my all, and it was hard, but not the kind of hard that I could do every day. The constant cleaning, the heat, the butt sweat."

"Butt sweat?"

"It's horrendous. No one tells you about that."

Ben couldn't help but laugh.

"You remember all those asinine conversations we used to have?" he grinned.

"Of course," Cynthia grinned back.

"I can see why the two of you were together," Esmee interjects again, reassuring the two that she is indeed still sitting there. Cynthia nods, keeping her mouth shut, her safest recourse.

Esmee continues while Ben is trying not to watch Cynthia across the table, fiddling with his silverware, his arm around another woman. The conversation is barely discernible above the energy that swirls between their silence.

Cynthia staves off feelings of remorse for the young woman. He does not love her. Or perhaps he does, but it pales in comparison to the current feelings Cynthia is now bringing up in him, which feels more like frustration than anything else.

He seemed to be grilling her about the past, testing her for consistency. She doesn't like being on the receiving end of the paranoia his father had wrought. He's likely regretting his decision to reach out as time wears on.

"Esmee, your mother's from Essex, isn't she?" Cynthia volunteers.

"She is."

"So's my grandmother. On my father's side."

"No shit!"

"I've been meaning to make a pilgrimage."

"You should, it's lovely. Oh, I'm so chuffed that we have so much in common!"

"Well... some things are a little awkward." Cynthia alludes.

"You know Benjamin's been engaged two other times. I think the third one is a charm, don't you, love? Ben says he thinks I'll be the one to stick."

"Remind me of the second one?" Cynthia says, ignoring a wave of nausea.

"The singer, with the Brazilian mum. A very long, elaborate prenup."

"The yellow diamond engagement ring," Cynthia nods.

"That's the one!" Esmee said. "He and I met at a charity function when they were together and... when they broke up, he called me."

"Romantic."

"Why didn't you propose to Cynthia, darling?"

"Because he was *already* engaged at the time," Cynthia fills in.

"Shocking!" Esmee gives him a reprimanding look.

"Can we please change the subject?" Ben groans.

"Nah," Cynthia wrinkles her nose.

"I think we can firmly establish Benjamin's type."

"What's that?"

"Ambitious women," Esmee innocently answers.

"I think you mean 'slightly colored' women," Cynthia replies, teasing him.

Ben looks up from the table at that, gives Esmee a laughing smirk, and looks back down again, as if faintly present but mostly pre-occupied. She grabs his chin and wiggles it.

"Is she your first colored girl, Ben?" Esmee teases him back.

"No," he says.

Cynthia's eyebrows go up in surprise.

"Really?"

He looks over at Cynthia's playful gaze, temporarily lifted out of his mood.

"I'm not rattling off my love life to the two of you."

"We want to know when this fetish of yours began, Benjamin."

"It's not a fetish."

"Slightly colored," Esmee repeats, snickering. Cynthia can't help but laugh as they both look over at him.

"I think I still pass the paper bag test," Cynthia boasts. The two women hold out their arms and compare their hues as if young girls again, instinctively turning their diamond-studded wrists palms up first, and then down, revealing the difference in their shades.

"You were in the oven a bit longer, yeah?" Esmee says, Cynthia nods.

"I'm very turned on right now," Ben confesses. The two

women laugh.

* * *

Cynthia parts ways with the couple after dinner and Ben is immediately hailing a cab.

"What's the matter, darling? Not feeling up to the walk? Are you aching again?"

"You could say that," he says with a mischievous grin as he grabs Esmee around her middle.

"You weren't kidding in there, were you?" Esmee giggles, moving her hands to his chest. He gives her a head-spinning kiss so intoxicating, that she doesn't even hear the sound of the cab pulling up.

They get in and Ben is instantly handsy, leaving Esmee to tell the clueless cabby where they are going.

"You cheeky boy," Esmee smiles. She looks into Ben's eyes, beckoning her wordlessly and she is surprised at him.

But then she stops. What are the odds that Ben is looking at her in a new way on the same night he happens to have dinner with a woman he "used to date"?

She stares and stares and watches as he looks back at her, oblivious. He's not even responding to her. She doesn't even need to be there.

"What?" he finally asks.

She wonders if she can take some other woman's love and be satisfied. She doesn't know if she can. Not because it would be beneath her, but because it would make her feel guilty.

She takes hold of his hand and moves it between her thighs, holding his gaze, waiting for an objection. They're less than a block away from home. But there's nothing less than that confident gaze in his eyes, the one he arrested her with when they first met.

His eyes dart back and forth between her eyes and her mouth. He licks his lips and she watches his jaw go a bit slack, a look she's never seen before. She takes hold of his arm, her wetness soaking his fingers. He rewards her arousal with a faster pace.

Dear God, is he imagining he's touching *her* right now?

The thought hits her brain and lights up her body's erogenous pathways like a subway map. Before she can second guess the impulse, she's climaxing in record time, breathing hard into his neck with a handful of his lapel in one fist.

The cab lurches to a stop, and before she can fully recover, Ben has a hold of her arm, plucking her from the cab and leading her up the front steps to their apartment on wobbly legs.

This is a problem, she thinks as they make their way up to the penthouse in the elevator.

"Get on your knees," Ben commands in a low panting voice, his hooded eyelids doing nothing to shield his gaze that has turned dark.

Tomorrow, she thinks, as she sinks down in front of him, her belly a churning storm of electric anticipation. She'll deal with this tomorrow.

* * *

Hours after their lovemaking Ben lies awake, long after Esmee has stopped pretending to be asleep, rolled over beside him. He stares up at the ceiling and sighs, a weight on his gut.

A house.

Strange how he never once wondered what she'd done with the money. He assumed she'd done what most people do with a paltry six figures. Certainly, some of it related to Indigo Properties. But essentially all of it had.

Extortion plus interest. His father paid to manipulate their lives. And with it, she forged an empire. It certainly went farther than he's ever seen hush money go. But it hadn't started that way.

Why had she been so elusive at work? Why had she jumped at the chance to stay at his apartment? Why would she betray him over money when she had access? To him? And why would she pour it all into a beat-up old house?

Because she had no house. At all.

Half-truths. That was his father's style. The Dvorak Group really had gotten her mother fired. And her house repossessed. If the "revenge plot" to get back at the company wasn't real, it should've been. Because he'd been too blind and privileged to notice that they had *never recovered.*

"I'm my own person now and I'll never have to make another deal like that again..."

The cramped mini-van. The leftover food that she faithfully gripped in her hand every night after work. Her refusal to bring her things to his place.

She simply bought her and her mother a place to live. A need so achingly simple and fundamental. A need she never trusted him to fill or understand.

And she was right not to.

9

Present Day

When Ben takes the short trek to his father's apartment, his heart nearly stops when he is greeted by Rosie at the door.

There is his father behind her, slightly stooped but still tall as ever, his curly salt and pepper hair now fully white and thinning up top. He is looking him square in the eye.

Ben freezes. His body turns cold.

Part of his brain is in denial, the other part is ready to be scolded. For something. For taking over the company.

There's something he's missed and his father has found out about it. It's something simple. He is about to be humiliated. Hundreds of employees will lose their jobs because of him.

And his father will only stare and stare, his eyes as bottomless as his and everyone else's debts. It will all come crashing down. Foreign countries will lose their wealth and its citizens will eat each other. And his father is staring and staring.

What is it, old man? For God's sake, he panics. The stare is as long as a year.

And then suddenly, it is over.

His father simply walks away, walking with purpose to another part of the room. He stops at a table, where he organizes papers. He then tears them up into squares. He moves with purpose to another part of the room.

Ben's eyes follow him everywhere. The sight is shocking. Humbling. His heart is still in his throat.

"He's never done *that* before," his sister Val's voice cuts through the surreal moment.

He looks over at his sister who looks ragged and worn. Dark circles are around her eyes.

"How long has he been like this?" Ben wonders.

"At least a week. All day. All night. He won't sleep at night."

"What the hell's wrong with him?"

"It's called Sundown Syndrome. Whatever's regulating his circadian rhythms is completely fucked."

"Won't he die if he doesn't sleep?"

"He's dying anyway. At least his brain is."

Ben lets out a sharp breath and shakes his head in disbelief. "This is fucking torture, Val. Weird, sick, psychological torture."

"It's nearly over."

"Put him in a facility Val."

"No."

"He sent us away when we were perfectly healthy. Don't you have a husband of your own that needs you? This is tearing you apart, I can see it."

"Do you remember the name of his sister? The one that died?"

"...No. Victoria? Vanessa?"

"Was it Ella?"

"No. It was 'v' something."

"He yells it sometimes. It's hard to restrain him and get him to calm down after that."

"Are you sure that's what he's even saying? Are you sure it's even a name?"

"Pretty sure. He keeps saying 'I'm sorry, I'm sorry.' It makes him cry."

"Val, you don't deserve this. To hear the broken, unfiltered contents of some sadistic person's mind? No one deserves this."

"That's exactly what I want," Val retorts. "That's exactly what I deserve. He recognizes me."

"What are you talking about?"

"Not all the time, but sometimes. He recognizes me, for the first time. Ever," she says, the tears immediately falling. "He tells me he loves me. He calls me his baby girl."

"Val, that's not him. He doesn't even talk like that," Ben insisted, "that's not him in there. He doesn't even know what he's saying."

"Sometimes he does. Sometimes it is. You can feel him come back. When you're around it long enough, you can start to feel it. The other day, I asked him if he knew how old he was and he said '30.' He didn't even hesitate. And then we had a good laugh about it."

"Jesus, Val."

"He knows what's happening to him, Ben. And he's scared. Like... he thinks he's already gone, but... then he comes back and he isn't. Every time it's like they're his last words. Completely stripped, no manipulation. I want to hear them. I want to hear every word."

* * *

Ben leaves his father's house completely drained, returning to work in a fog. Between last night's dinner and what he's just witnessed, he feels an urgent dread in his gut, like he's done something terrible and he's about to be called into the headmaster's office. And it would be a lot less terrifying if he knew what he's done to land him there. He stares absentmindedly at his desk. His assistant's voice interrupts his stupor.

"Sir, you had a reporter from the Tribune call while you were out, wanting a statement on the recent article about Evan Bolinger, and also CNN is still waiting on the okay regarding their previous interview."

"Not now."

"Can I give them a timeline?"

"Fuck, Lisa. Tomorrow, alright? Before noon."

"Thank you, sir. Also, I've got Dev for you on line 2."

"Dev? What does he want?"

"He says he's having trouble with a high priority client."

"Which client?"

"He didn't specify."

Ben picked up line 2.

"Dev."

"Boss. I just talked to Dale Abernathy."

"About?"

"He wants to buy an island."

"What?"

"He's getting married or something... his assistant says he found an island near Santorini."

"What's the problem?"

"He wants to buy it and build on it. Like within the next two weeks."

Ben shook his head with a shrug. "...I'm still missing the plot here."

"He's paying me to advise him. Should I tell him it's a dumb fuckin' idea?"

"You should absolutely not do that."

"But it is a dumb fuckin' idea, isn't it?"

"Of course it is."

"Okay. Just wanted to make sure I wasn't losing my mind," Dev sighed.

"Look, Dale doesn't hire yes men, so tell him what you think. Because if he even smells that you're blowing smoke up his ass, I'm gonna get a phone call."

"So?"

"So, tell him the truth."

"If I tell him the truth, and it works out anyway, then I'm a shitty advisor. If I tell him the truth and it doesn't work out, then I'm a shitty advisor.

"All in the delivery. Just don't be a buzzkill. Tell him that it's a dumb fuckin' idea, but what the hell, it's his money and you only live once. He can fuckin' buy Greece, he'll still have enough to retire. Not in those words, but you get it."

"Sir, Cynthia Gordon is here for your 2:00," Lisa chimed in.

"I gotta go Dev, are we done here?"

"Did I just hear the name 'Cynthia Gordon'?" Dev grinned.

"It's a long fucking story. Later, Dev. Try not to lose our single most important client."

"No pressure."

* * *

As she returns to the Dvorak building for the first time in ten years, Cynthia takes a deep breath. She arrives outside the familiar office, the one that changed her life a decade earlier.

She was still in her work uniform the last time she was called up here. She smelled like french fries. She could feel the grease on her skin and she felt strange sitting on the tufted black leather couch in the waiting room that was softer than anything she'd slept on in over a year. Aside from Benji's bed. He used to make fun of her, how long she would sleep when she was over. He would come home from work and she was still asleep.

There wasn't anything about the job that warranted her seeing the damn CEO anyway. Silly how she hadn't realized that. Even if she'd burned the whole place down, he would've had people to deal with that.

She scoffs at the memory. He must've seen her coming from a mile away.

She is in the same waiting room now. The furniture is different. Less comfortable. Aside from the new carpet, it's virtually the same, down to the layout. It's in desperate need of a makeover.

"I'm a huge fan of your work, by the way," Ben's assistant suddenly blurts.

"You've seen my work?"

"You did Mr. Manchester's place. We had our Christmas party at their house in the Hamptons. And Farm to Table downtown, of course."

"Of course. Thank you, very much."

"I heard you used to work here."

"A million years ago. In the kitchen."

"Dev still raves about your food. We all call him Dev. He insists."

"How is Dev?"

"Lisa, send her in," Ben is heard over her intercom.

"Mr. Dvorak will see you now," his assistant says as she got up from her desk. She's young. No particular feelings of jealousy or suspicion radiating from her. She can't tell if Ben has ever slept with her or not.

Lisa leads her into Ben's office which is just as large and overwhelming as she remembers. Much fewer people in it this time. The grand cherry wood desk remains in place. As she would imagine. He probably has a sentimental attachment to his father's desk. Naturally, he would want it to be his as well. They made love on it once. She couldn't stop staring at it the day they sacked her. She kept thinking to herself that there was no way his father would've known what they had done. No way he would be sitting at it so confidently as if he owned it, if he knew.

"You kept the desk," she says, instantly addressing the room's elephant.

"It's cumbersome to get rid of. It would have to be dismantled. Carried down 27 flights of stairs. Too big to fit in an elevator. Hell, too big to fit through one of these windows and turn it into firewood."

"I wonder how many more times it was christened since you became the president."

He gives her a heart-melting smile that tells her he's pleased that she brought it up. He gives her a slow once over as he gestures for her to sit down, admiring her posh-looking turquoise dress with the embellishment on one shoulder.

"Do you? Wonder?"

"Sure," Cynthia volunteers, as if her curiosity is common. "Have you had your way with young Lisa out there?"

"Not yet," he chuckles.

"Waiting for the right time?"

"Typically, I sleep with them first, and then I hire them."

"Unorthodox."

"They don't last very long."

"So you thought you'd try it the other way?"

"Lisa's my cousin," he smirks with a sigh.

"How far removed?"

He can't stifle a laugh.

"The one time I sleep with the staff..." Ben shakes his head.

"Thank you for dinner, by the way. Your fiancée seems lovely."

"Nosy, you mean."

"Not at all."

"Feels like we didn't get a proper chance to catch up," he says provocatively, at least in her estimation. He gives her a burning look that makes her stomach sickly drop.

Just when it seemed like they were going to manage some sort of platonic balance. She wants to know what happened but she's afraid to ask. *Just say the word, girl,* is what his eyes seem to be saying.

His office is three times the size of hers and has a bathroom with a shower. He's exuding every inch of his CEO power and they're a hundred feet in the air. Her blood gallops through her veins, heated. She's startled enough by her reaction to his benign statement that she's starting to wonder if she's simply projecting.

"...I'm sorry we didn't get a proper chance to talk *design* choices," she skillfully segues with a clear of her throat. "I brought sketches."

Ben's sigh sounds exasperated. He rubs his brow. "I'm sure they're beautiful."

"You don't want to see them?"

"I keep telling you that I trust your taste."

"Honestly, Benjamin what am I here for, then?"

"Our assistants scheduled this meeting, not me."

Cynthia sighs.

"I came all the way here."

"I'm sure it was just like the Oregon trail."

"I had blueprints made."

"Money's no object, like I said."

"Look at the fuckin' sketches, Benji."

He smiles. He's wondered if he would ever hear that nickname again.

"Fine," he concedes, summoning them over the wide desk with a long arm. Cynthia retrieves the sketches and arranges them in a line across from him wordlessly.

"They're beautiful," he says, clearly feigning enthusiasm.

Cynthia shoots him an arresting look of shock at his callous response. Ben returns her gaze stoically, a tug of war between remorse and amusement within him. Amusement was winning.

"So arrogant," Cynthia shakes her head. "You buy my time just so you can waste it?"

"I saw my father today."

Cynthia pauses.

"How is he?"

"Not good. He's usually in his room when I go over there. For my sake, mostly. The last time I talked to him, he was ranting and raving. Saying awful things. And it would get more and more jumbled. But now... he hardly talks. He wanders around aimlessly. It's much more frightening."

"I'm so sorry, Ben," she offers her sympathies freely. Openly. For his father. He fights off annoyance.

"Never mind. It's... I'm just pre-occupied. I could give a shit about fixtures. Honest to God."

"I understand. I'll make the executive decisions, I suppose. Still..."

"What?"

117

"You could've canceled the meeting."

"Not a chance. I'd never turn down an excuse to see you."

Cynthia's eyes narrow on Ben. She remains in her cross-legged position across from him. She sends him a warning shot, weary of playing games.

"Ben, what is this? What are you doing?"

"At this moment, I'm being honest."

"Benji, you're confused. At best. Parading that poor girl around, like you're going to marry her," Cynthia casually confides. Yet Ben stiffens as though she has overstepped her bounds.

"I *am* going to marry her."

She's going to scream. Right in his face until he's deaf.

"Why? Because she makes you happy?"

"No."

Ben doesn't elaborate and Cynthia just gives him a brief airy laugh.

"...Well? I'm on the edge of my seat."

"I'm not marrying for love, Cynth. I can't."

"Why's that?"

"Because it would just be cruel. I work like a maniac. And honestly... I don't care. I just don't want to be alone."

"That's... sad as fuck, Ben," Cynthia scoffs, careful not to sound anything but objective.

"*You* wanna get married?"

"Eventually."

"To whom?"

"His name is Curtis," she says with a straight face, dramatically. Ben grins, knowing it's sarcasm. And also that she's not seeing *anyone* at the moment.

"Do *you* wanna marry me? I'll call it off right now."

Yes.

"Sorry, if 'I can't marry for love,' and 'I don't care. I just don't wanna be alone,' doesn't make me swoon," she says with faint indignance.

"Walked right into that one," he grins, feeling a little gross. It was a joke, but also not. Perhaps the shittiest shot he's ever taken, on the person who deserved a whole lot more.

"Does Esmee know you feel this way?" she asks.

"Why do you even care?" he suddenly snaps. *Ugh.* Maybe he should've canceled. Cynthia doesn't let him off the hook.

"So now I don't care about you? Because I didn't accept your shitty proposal?"

"I didn't say that. Clearly, you've moved on. To houses. So don't worry about me, I'll be fine."

"Believe it or not, I care about your... stability, Ben."

"I think I heard more about you last night than I ever have."

"That's not true."

"You never talked about yourself. With me. "

"...Sure I did."

"You didn't. Not once," he says. His tone borders accusation. Cynthia gives him a shrug in response, barely noticing.

"I've never been the type to go on and on about myself. Still aren't. Your girlfriend is simply more inquisitive than most people."

"We never talked about anything of substance."

"We both liked asinine conversations. If you didn't know it's because you didn't ask."

Ben resented the implication. "I did, but I knew better than to push. It was years before I realized you never actually opened up. You gave me nothing."

Cynthia licked her lips. Maybe he had a point, but it was all he had.

"So now it's my fault? You're telling me if I were more self-absorbed, you would've fought for me, is that it?"

"Perhaps you had something to hide," he eyes her. "Perhaps you liked to keep me talking."

"Or maybe you were short on people that genuinely cared about you, and I was sympathetic to that. Maybe you were using me. Maybe I was the only one risking anything by getting close to you since I could be kicked out on my ass if it all went south. And you would just... keep being a Dvorak."

Cynthia calmly eyes him back as she reads him his rights, which are exactly none. He huffs a laugh, absent-mindedly fiddling with his mont blanc fountain pen.

"Fair enough," he answers sheepishly. He used to think she had this chip on her shoulder. But knowing the truth, it seemed it deserved to be there.

He can't believe she's still too stubborn to even mention ever being homeless, as if it didn't matter. Even now she can't admit to him that she ever needed his help. He did not share her handicap.

"Can't remember the last time I had one of those," Ben says. He doesn't elaborate.

"What?"

"An asinine conversation," he nods, somewhat pitifully, in response.

Cynthia feels a pang of guilt. He'd once told her she was his best friend. It was sad then, and she was remembering it now. Watching him sitting alone in this stark corner office, she realizes that he never found a new best friend. The notion twists her sympathies.

He misses her, Cynthia realizes. Not everything has to be

about riling her up and pushing her buttons and battering her defenses.

She supposes she can indulge him for an afternoon. After this, there would be very little need for them to meet up again, if at all. Surely she can keep herself from saying too much for *one* meeting.

"We could've had our own MeTv Channel by now," she offers diplomatically.

He sits back in his chair, grinning. "We would've definitely been internet famous."

10

Ten Years Ago

"I remember when I first found out that my penis actually went in something."

Cynthia died laughing as she lay next to him on the couch in his apartment. His apartment was only 900 square feet, which was slumming it for him. But it was convenient.

It had all the sparse trappings of bachelorhood. He was hella privileged, but he was still taking care of himself, with his own money, for the first time. And it was exhilarating.

They were days away from sleeping with each other and it showed. Their conversations became strange and penetrating, if not meandering.

"I was so, so happy. It was probably the equivalent of... finding out World War I was ending."

Cynthia couldn't catch her breath.

"When was this?" she asked when she finally recovered.

"I was probably about... eleven."

"Wow, that's early."

"Is it? It would be a few years before the dream became a reality."

"How many?"

"Not telling."

"You should know by now I wouldn't make fun of you."

"I know."

"You tell me everything else."

"I know."

"Speaking of discovering sex, I think I had a sort of similar moment to yours, except my reaction was the exact opposite."

Ben covered both his hands with his face as a rare sympathy for girls washed over him.

"That must've sounded like a horror movie plot."

"I didn't believe it at *all*, at first."

"Oh, Cynth."

"And then my friend— the one who told me— got this like, encyclopedia from her parents' room, opened it up to this diagram."

"And there it was," Ben filled in.

"There it was."

"How'd it make you feel?"

"Like... one day life as you knew it would be over. Which was true, but it wasn't a good feeling. It was like this countdown began. How many days do I have left?"

"Of childhood," he filled in as though he understood.

"Yeah. My first experience was... not so good. I blame the diagram."

"I'm sure the guy deserves some of the blame."

"For sure."

"Imagine if you'd been told it was going to be the best experience of your life, though."

"That happens to a lot of girls, actually."

"When was this first experience of yours, if you don't mind

my asking?"

"Um... last year."

He tried not to act terribly surprised. Or disappointed. A measly six months between her choosing that bastard over him.

"Last year? No shit. Boyfriend?"

"No," she cryptically answered. "What about you?"

"My first?"

"Yeah. Was it everything you'd been dreaming?"

He groaned as he rolled over on his side, not facing her. She laughed in anticipation.

"More. One might say it was *too* good."

"Oh no," she winced in sympathy as if she was his mom. Which made him feel worse.

"That reaction is...not helping me."

She laughed, "Was it a world record?"

"Yes. And then I cried."

"Oh, Benji," she said as if he were adorable. She rubbed his arm.

"I've never told anyone that."

"Such a sensitive soul, you are."

"I think you meant to say 'sensitive ween.'"

Cynthia laughed.

"Why do you like hangin' out with me?" she asked.

"Isn't it obvious?"

"No."

"We have nothing in common," he said.

"That's the reason?"

"And because you agreed to it. And you're beautiful. And I like you. I can talk to you."

His words resounded all along the insides of her like she was an instrument his words could pluck. She was barely out of high school and she couldn't have been more flattered. He seemed so achingly mature.

"You a *battyman,* awat?" Cynthia asked in a rare display of Grenadian patois.

"A what?" he smiled.

"Are you *gay.*"

"I just bared my heterosexual soul to you," he chuckled.

"It's just weird that you haven't tried to sleep with me, I guess."

"I haven't?" he smiled.

"No."

"How do *you* know?"

"I'm well-versed in seduction," she giggled.

"Anyway, you seem disappointed," he replied looking over at her. His arm was laying above his head. His voice barely a whisper, his eyes full of stars that she didn't notice. Cynthia was examining the cotton blend of his gray t-shirt.

"Not disappointed just... confused," she said, "some days it seems like you want to, but still. You don't."

"You think I go around doing everything I want to do?" he asked. She couldn't tear her eyes away from his t-shirt. It was as though she felt time slow down and she thought, *so, this is how it feels. Right before he asks and you say yes.*

"Well, yeah. I do. And I don't have the advantages you have."

He sighed, straightening his head and looking up at the ceiling. "Advantages. These advantages you speak of are... Faustian."

"Faustian?"

"The Faustian Deal. Heard of it?"

"Like, a deal with the devil?"

"Basically. You sell your soul for fame, or money, or power. Then you become famous, for something you hate. You make

125

money and lose everyone you love. You gain power, but it's in hell."

"What deal did you make?"

"None. As far as I can tell. I was born into it. I didn't get to choose."

"So? Leave it all behind. You're young. There's still time to back out."

The way she said it so flippantly. As though it were simple, a matter of flicking your wrist. This must be what poor people were always complaining about.

"That's the thing. I don't think I could survive."

"Sure you could. You could if you had to," she continued her optimistic rant.

"Maybe I'm afraid. You ever think of that?"

"Afraid of what?"

"I'm afraid I'll embarrass myself."

"You can't do any worse than your first time."

"I wouldn't count on it."

Cynthia chuckles, conspicuously quiet. His forearm found the warmth of her back.

"I like you. A lot. I feel… a connection with you."

"Which is what guys say when they want to sleep with you."

"True."

"Where's your girlfriend when I'm here with you?" she asked.

The prospect sent zings straight to his groin. He shifted his weight, chuckling nervously as he fought off a boner.

"She's… somewhere. Over-achieving. She was born into it the same way I was. She's much more adapted to it than I am."

"How do you feel about that?"

"I… don't… feel anything about that."

"How long have you been together?"

"Three years. No, four years."

"Do you love her?" Cynthia asked. She was simply after his honesty. He found the question challenging.

"I... I don't know."

"How do you not know?"

"It's complicated, Cynth. Love isn't like the movies."

"Sure it is. Why else would people make movies about it?"

He laughed at her response that was equal parts naive and wise. "I... have no rebuttal," he said. "Anyway, I'm not even sure I'm capable of that kind of love. It's so volatile. Melanie and I at least agree on that front. Her parents are happy, my parents are happy, it works."

"So basically it's an arranged marriage."

"Well... not really. We chose each other. At least, I think we did," Ben smirked, ignoring the gnawing paranoia Cynthia's words conceived in him.

"...You think I'm beautiful?"

He scoffed. "Honestly, what is up with beautiful women always asking that? Like they don't know?"

"Are we never going to know what it's like to kiss?" Cynthia whispered. In her head, it sounded like a bullhorn.

He sighed as he took one of her hands, and kissed it.

He couldn't. He entertained the glorious disaster in his mind, of his plans and the plans of those closest to him completely coming apart.

And yet, part of him wanted to give her hope. And for some reason, it didn't feel like a lie.

"We will," he answered. "Someday we will."

* * *

Only one week later Ben arrived at work, terribly distracted. He didn't leave his office. No way he was going down to the cafeteria today.

He'd crossed the line with Cynthia that morning before he left for work. She was sleeping in his big bed. He slept on the couch as usual, but he had to pass her on the way to his shower, and when he got dressed.

Cynthia's workday started a few hours later than his. Every once in a while, he would come out of the shower and watch her sleep. Or he would finish dressing and he would watch her fondly, snickering at the way she slept like a rock. This morning, she'd done something she'd never done before. She woke up.

Ben emerged from his closet to see her clear eyes meeting his, and she broke into a smile as she raised up her head and rested it on her elbow. He melted.

"What time is it?"

"Almost 7."

She stretched, looking for a moment like she would turn over and go back to sleep. Instead, she sat up, wearing one of his dress shirts since she refused to bring her things over.

Something either came over him or lifted off of him. He sauntered over to her side of the bed and sat down, her body between his and his propped arm. Her hair was a bit messy. She'd dyed it a dark red a few days ago. Before that, it was blue at the tips. Despite the daring color, there was still something classic and demure about her appearance. He looked into her eyes as he smiled.

"See you tonight?" he said, not having much of a reason to even be talking to her right now, let alone draped over her in bed. He imagined for a moment that she was his.

"Yup," she nodded, cracking a smile. She seemed to be doing

the same.

"Okay," he answered needlessly.

"'kay," she replied softly.

And then he moved in close. His head leaned in left, she went right, and slowly, their lips touched. A perfect kiss for a perfect moment. It was so perfect in fact, that he didn't even need more.

"Bye."

"Bye."

He walked out of the apartment with a spring in his step and stopped in the middle of the hallway, wrestling with himself. Surprisingly his intellect won out and he continued on his way to work.

All day his computer screen blurred in front of him as he was lost in thought.

"So, rumor has it Cynthia's got a boyfriend."

Ben pretended not to hear.

"*Dammit.* Who?"

"Don't know. I think it's someone in the kitchens."

Ben gave a smirk.

"Ben, you're awfully quiet. Anything to confess?"

"Why me?"

"Everyone knows you took her up to Princeton. Any extra-curriculars happen?"

"No. We're just friends."

"She hasn't told you about a boyfriend?"

"No."

"Pretty sure there's a policy about the staff dating. She could seriously get fired for that."

"Yeah, it's called the Declan policy."

The guys laughed. Declan Smith was a Junior VP who'd allegedly gotten one of the maids pregnant a few years ago.

"Nothing wrong with kitchen staff dating each other," Ben said, knowing the rule since he'd looked it up himself. "Technically we shouldn't be tangled up with the staff's personal lives at all. It screams 'lawsuit.'"

"Something about poor kitchen wenches gets me all hot and bothered," Leland said. Ben didn't know much about Leland, but it seemed like he was always trying to prompt Ben to talk about his personal life, so he probably worked for his father. Ben had been meaning to tell his dad to get someone a little less eager next time if he were trying to get any real information, but why give him the advantage?

"Who's the source of this 'rumor' anyway?" Ben feigned interest.

"Dev said he saw her leaving with someone after work a few times."

Ben stiffened. The room practically disappeared and words faded into the background noise.

Cynthia got off at five. Much earlier than him. Early enough to have a guy in and out of his place without him being the wiser.

Was Cynthia bringing other guys to his place while he was at work?

Other 'guys' plural? Really? the voice in his brain snarked. Meanwhile, his imagination was flooding with images of Cynthia running a brothel while he was gone.

Okay, maybe it was just one guy. He'd given her a key, and virtually no stipulations. It's not like they were together. They weren't. At least, they weren't supposed to be.

He was sort of getting used to her as a roommate. And she was a good one. She cleaned up. She brought home take-out and always had just enough left for him to scarf up on the days he skipped lunch.

Maybe there was one guy. She was allowed to have a guy. He himself had a girlfriend. Nay, a fiancée. He told himself he'd been honest with Cynthia, but he'd never been able to describe Melanie as anything but a girlfriend.

Which was the lie? That Melanie was only a girlfriend or the fact that, after meeting Cynthia, he ever intended to marry Melanie?

He'd caught Melanie cheating once. With one of his best friends during summer break, right before he proposed. She cried, he cried, and when he agreed to take her back, she was sobbing with elation. The relationship with his best friend was doomed, but he figured if he and Melanie could survive that, they could survive marriage.

But now he realized that he couldn't marry Melanie. Because even though he'd given Cynthia the title friend, roommate, co-worker, and every other title that existed *besides* girlfriend, the very thought that she could even be looking into another man's eyes without him knowing was causing him such anguish, such emotional discomfort, that he was resolved to leave early and confront her before she walked in the door.

He'd never felt that for another woman. And now that he knew that he could, he realized he was in a real quagmire. He couldn't imagine a future without Melanie, but he didn't want to imagine the present without Cynthia.

* * *

"Are you bringing guys here?"

"What?"

Cynthia walked in the door of Ben's apartment, startled to find him already there on the couch when he had hours left on his shift.

"Dev said he saw you with some guy at work?"

"Oh, that's just... my boss. We used to work at this steakhouse not that far from here, so we were getting together with some of our old co-workers. He's the one that hired me when he got the job here—"

"Dev said there was more than one."

Cynthia's heart beat faster, but only because Ben was being so confrontational. She tried not to read too much into it, in case she was paranoid.

"Dev?" she furrowed her brow, "why wouldn't you just ask me?"

"Because if you're bringing guys here, you may not want to be truthful with me about it."

"...I'm not, nor would I ever, bring a guy here."

"Okay."

"Okay."

"I don't care who you sleep with," Ben added, "I just care if you're using my resources to do it."

She didn't know which part of his sentence to hate more.

"Well, like I said... I'm not, nor would I ever bring a guy here."

"So you *are* sleeping with someone?"

Was this a joke?

"When would I even have time to do something like that?" Cynthia asked dumbfounded.

"I don't know what you do on your days off. I'm at work 7 days a fuckin' week."

"Well, my mom does occasionally like to see me."

"I'm not keeping you from your mom."

"I didn't say you... Ben, what is this?"

"I just need to know if you're running some kind of scam—"

"Because I'm poor and black and I work in a kitchen? What, I'm too young to graduate college, but I know the ins and outs of scamming?"

"Why are you bringing race into this?"

"Because I'm poor and I work in a kitchen, then? Which part of me should I blame this *ridiculous* conversation on?"

"That would be your tits."

"Since when have you seen my tits?"

"I haven't."

Cynthia put her hands up slowly as though she were dealing with an escaped mental patient. "Look, you're obviously talking crazy and having paranoid delusions, so I'm just gonna go."

"Great. I'll be needing that key, before you leave."

Shit. Did he think she meant for good? He was kicking her out?

God. Rich guys are the *worst*.

She stopped for a second, exasperated and ready to clarify that she only needed to go for a walk.

But why bother? If he could do this to her at the drop of a hat, then she didn't need it. She hated finding out that her relationship with Ben was so unstable.

She reached in her pocket for the lonely key that he'd given her. She used to have a set. A little ugly old Geo Metro she got for a few hundred bucks. She and her friends used to smoke weed in it. Her house keys, of course. A key to the garage apartment she was going to move into once she graduated.

But those were long gone. She had nothing in her pockets but lint. It's not like she considered Ben's apartment home, but she never dreamed that life entailed so many instances of giving away keys to things that were once yours to have.

She lobbed the key at his head before she walked out of the

front door and left it wide open.

"Shit!" Ben launched himself off the couch the minute Cynthia was gone, bracing himself for the uncomfortable bramble down the stairs he was going to have to do to catch up with her.

How the hell did he just let that stupid moment happen? By the time he got to the hallway, Cynthia was already on her way down the elevator. He made his way painfully down to the lobby, where she was nearly out the door.

"Cynthia!" he yelled.

He went outside, where he was freezing. He suddenly noticed Cynthia was wearing only a small bomber jacket. Why didn't she just stop being stubborn and bring more of her things?

Oh, I don't know, Ben. Maybe she was worried you would kick her out without warning like a madman, he thought. God, why was he doing all the wrong things?

"Cynthia, stop," he yelled behind her as she walked.

She wouldn't stop.

Shit. His apartment door was wide open. But he couldn't turn back. Not if Cynthia wasn't coming with him.

He caught up enough with her to grab her by the wrist and she stopped, visibly shaken and unwilling to turn and face him. She was kidding herself if she thought she could be prideful right now. Her mom was in the woman's shelter for 50 and older, a clean one, where she was safe. Where exactly could she go? To sleep on the subway?

He grabbed her hand and she sobbed a little louder as she sheepishly followed behind him, the New Yorkers passing by thankfully minding their business as he led her back to his place. The scene of a well-dressed Ben unapologetically waddling down the street with a crying black girl in tow was probably just strange enough to earn their respect. Still, a few guys couldn't help have an excuse to impress the cute girl with the pale ocean eyes.

"You aight ma?" one of them said. She nodded in response.

He dragged her all the way back to his building, up the stairs and into his apartment, onto the couch. The door was still wide open when they both flopped down, Cynthia's intermittent sniffs still adorning the silence.

He looked at her dainty, wheat-colored hands in her lap holding a balled-up tissue, a cheap burgundy on her fingernails. Her jeans against the fabric of his tufted leather. She was still wearing her flimsy bomber jacket. He stared and stared as though his memory depended on it, his mind empty. Suddenly he spoke.

"I don't want you to leave. I don't know why I said that."

Cynthia was quiet.

"Actually I do know why I said it. I was angry. Jealous. I was crazy jealous."

Cynthia swallowed, feeling as though she were drowning. He kept his eyes glued to the empty space between them.

"I don't have a boyfriend. Why would I let you kiss me?" she said, as though that were proof.

"I let you kiss me. And I have a girlfriend."

"Well, I'm not like you, Ben. You don't even know if you *love* your girlfriend. And you have the nerve to be jealous? At least I know that I have no right to you whatsoever."

"I know that I have no right to you. That's why... look, I don't want you to leave, okay? If you wanna bring other guys over—"

"I don't want to bring other guys over!" Cynthia cried.

"Maybe not now, I'm just saying in the future..."

"In the future? How long do you think I'm staying here?"

"I... I don't know. I don't want to know. I just... I want you to feel welcome. I do. And I listened to my idiot co-workers, and it... caught me off guard, that's all. I started freaking out that you were just taking me for a ride."

"You're so vulnerable, Ben," Cynthia sneered sarcastically.

Ben sighed as he sat back. He took hold of one of Cynthia's hands, palms up, caressing her fingers. His front door was still wide open, right off the kitchen. A few passers-by fought the temptation to stop to look inside as they slowly passed. Cynthia's breathing slowed. Her nipples tightened against her chest as Ben unknowingly stimulated the nerves across her fingers, skimming her skin. She began nervously to talk, to cover her erratic breathing.

"So, I've been meaning to ask you. And I guess this is as good a time as any. I've been here nearly a month. If you want, I could start paying rent here."

"No, you couldn't," he scoffed.

"Let me pay something. Anything."

"Not a chance."

"Look, it's not like I want things to change, well... I mean... I feel the same way, in a way, I guess, it's just—"

"I know," he said, looking down at some mysterious point of interest, his long lashes shielding his dark brown eyes.

"Know what?" Cynthia breathed, not even sure what she meant by her ramble. He still had her palm in his.

"I feel it too, I'm not an idiot," he scoffed.

"So... what do we do?" she asked in a rasp.

He sighed again, as though looking at a confusing puzzle in the lines of her palm that his life was dependent on solving.

"I don't know."

"Are you going to kiss me again?"

"I think so."

She watched his brow furrowed, his brown eyes studying the brown-colored branches of indentions in her hands, looking past them.

"Just kiss me, Ben."

Ben huffed a laugh.

"That won't solve anything it'll just... cause more problems."

"Then I should leave."

"...So you're blackmailing me?"

"I'm trying to help you. And myself."

"*Fuck.*"

"Just *kiss* me! Ben!"

"Cynthia, I'm not gonna 'just *kiss* you'!" he answered, exasperated. "If I start, I'm not gonna stop at '*kissing*'!"

"Good!" she exclaimed.

Ben sighed, Cynthia's enthusiastic reply only fanning the flames under his roasting conscience.

"Cynthia, I'm a cheater. Already. If I do that, it makes me just as bad as her."

"She cheated on you?"

"...Once."

"...So you're in a relationship with a cheating woman that you don't love..."

"Cynthia, enough. You don't... it's complicated okay?"

"This isn't fair, Benji."

"I know."

"I'm going to take a shower. I smell like vegetable oil."

Cynthia retreated to the bathroom, shedding her jacket and uniform while the water heated, frustrated more by Ben's actions than her living situation. He wasn't lying, he was genuinely unsure.

Stupid rich weirdos and their girlfriends. She couldn't deny his insistence on being faithful made her both love and hate Ben, *and* this Melanie chick. The idea that he wanted her back... she wished she just had the strength to walk away. For both their sakes.

Suddenly there was a knock at the bathroom door.

Cynthia startled, naked and about to wash off the day. She grabbed a towel and slowly began wrapping it around herself before she stopped. She dropped the towel and took a deep breath before slowly opening the door.

Instantly she was confronted with Ben's raw gaze, his audible breath heavy, his eyes never leaving hers as though afraid to venture any lower. She opened the door wider and he slowly limped his way inside, closing the door behind him and leaning up against it. Finally, he let himself take in the sight of her pert breasts, her brown nipples.

His hands went to starch white of his shirt buttons, undoing them one by one, revealing his undershirt. Hers went to his belt buckle, her hair in a long, choppy dark red bob, long bangs framing her face.

Gingerly he stepped out of his pants, letting Cynthia peel them down over his legs pinching themselves together. She was surprised to see they were pale and a bit muscular at the calves and thighs. Unusually weak-looking in other places, covered in scars presumably from surgeries.

He went from semi-erect to rock hard right before her eyes. She pressed herself against him as she stood upright. Ben was breathing so hard with his hands at his sides as if paralyzed. She reached up on tiptoes, closed her eyes, and kissed his lips. Their tongues slowly intertwined, again and again between kisses until they were dizzy.

"Cynthia?"

"What?" she replied, reaching for the elastic on his boxers.

"I'm sorry that I couldn't be your first," he whispered.

"Benji..."

Ben responded with his lips fiercely on hers again. A hand went to the side of her face. They kissed and kissed until finally she broke away from him, grabbed him by the hand, and led him into the shower stall, Ben watching her bare shoulders and back as she moved in front of him, their mismatched hands lazily intertwined.

11

Present Day

Esmee is back in town after two weeks in some location he hasn't bothered to remember. If she hadn't sent a text, he would've gone straight home to his apartment after work, rather than meet her at her hotel, her semi-permanent home away from home.

"Want to make love, my dear?"

"I'm really exhausted."

"It's just that I leave for Prague on Monday. I'd like to have as much of you as I can before I leave."

"I know. Me too. If I could, I would. You know that. But I had a long day today and another tomorrow. Stopping by to see Val and then Cynthia right after."

"Val? Don't you mean your father?"

"No."

"You know, I wouldn't mind going with you once, to see him. It wouldn't frighten me if that's what you're worried about."

"I'm not."

"How's Cynthia, then?"

"She's good."

"Please send her my love. We had such a lovely dinner the other night. I miss her. Will you tell her?"

"I will."

And like that, Esmee is back in "three words maximum" hell. She can't think of what she's said to land herself there and never knows how to get out.

"Is the house nearly done? I'm afraid I'll be gone before I see the finished product."

"You will, unfortunately."

"It'll be good once it's done. Seeing your old flame seems to take a lot out of you, darling. More than seeing your father, I think."

"It does," Ben admitted, without elaborating.

"I could tell at dinner that you were both a great deal pent up. And I'm English."

Ben merely huffed an appreciative laugh.

"I hope you manage to get everything off your chest in the little time you have left with her, because you've really become quite the martyr since she re-appeared. Call me jealous, but I think she's still in love with you."

Ben didn't answer at all.

"...Or is it the other way around?"

"Esmee, enough."

"...Love, you promised me we would always be honest with each other."

"Yes, and honestly, I don't want to talk about this. With anyone."

"Not even with me?"

"Especially not with you."

More than three words. At least she's made it out of hell. And in record time.

"At least now I know the reason you don't seem to adore me. For a moment I thought perhaps you were homosexual."

Ben just sighs in the darkness.

"Well. Seems you can't bring yourself to hate me either. Honestly, darling I'm relieved. This, I can deal with. This, I understand."

Ben caught the stench of manipulation in her words, the desire for control over him, even if it was only perceived. He was nearly sick with deja vu.

"I meant what I said about not wanting to talk about this, Esmee."

"Of course, darling."

"Great."

"...Good night, then," Esmee sweetly responds. Ben knows it's her polite English version of a protest. If they can't talk about this, then they wouldn't talk about anything. Which suited him fine.

"Good night."

* * *

The next morning, Esmee is already gone when he wakes. He showers, feeling relieved that she has chosen to give him the space that he often requests from her. He decides that he'll have to make it up to her tonight, with dinner. Meanwhile, he braces himself for his afternoon meeting with Cynthia, likely one of his last.

When Ben shows up at his property on Moss Lane, men in boots are crawling all over the place like giant ants. He lets out a deep sigh from his car as he looks at his little project coming right along.

142

Not a cloud in the sky, no shipment delays, no emergency pipe bursts to call about. No need to design for the client, since he was selling. No budget concerns to brief him on, he certainly made sure of that.

While he is grateful that they've managed to regain some level of rapport, now their time is almost through and they've barely scratched the surface of what was really on his mind.

He honestly doesn't quite know what it is. All he knows is that his mouth still feels burdened, his ears unsatisfied. As it is, he's lucky to see her once a week or talk to her for ten minutes.

He shows up on the day that the meager master bedroom window is in the midst of being transformed into an intimate balcony area that juts out like a lip, as though it'd always been there. He walks through the open front door by way of the newly constructed porch, her signature Southern-style influence that seemed to infect every Gordon creation. He finds her immediately, with an old sweat sock on her hand and several cans of stain in front of her as she sits on the newly stripped stairs.

"So? What do you think?" she chirps without looking up.

"It's... coming along."

"Coming along? That's all you have to say?"

"I'm honestly impressed. Something about it feels... very grand already. You've pulled out all the stops."

Cynthia smiles. "Couldn't very well waste an unlimited budget now, could I? Did you see the balcony?"

"I did."

"Ask me how much."

He laughs. He could care less, but he can't resist humoring her. A cup of coffee was still around five dollars these days, wasn't it?

"Ten thousand," he throws out.

"Jesus!"

"That's what I'd pay for a balcony like that."

"Okay, fair enough. It does add a lot of value."

"Don't keep me in suspense, Cynth," he says. She grins.

"Five. hundred. dollars," she dramatically discloses.

"Get out!" he feigns wonder.

"It's impressive and you know it," she says in a reprimanding tone.

"It is," he concedes. "Don't you have people for this?" he nods towards the stain cans strewn about her.

"Having your 'people' select the stain for your stairs is like hiring someone to masturbate yourself."

"It's a thing," Ben defends his position, smiling.

"Perhaps, but it garners mixed results. This has to be done right."

"Isn't it all done right, Miss Gordon?"

"Let me rephrase: this has to be done *perfectly.*"

Ben looks down at his shoes and puts his hands in his pockets before he launches into his final chest-baring attempt. "So it seems our professional relationship is swiftly coming to a close."

Cynthia wrinkles her brow. "I suppose."

"Care to talk about more ancient history?"

"I don't. But I take it you do?" Cynthia groans, popping open the can of walnut colored stain.

"My father told me that you had it out for him. For what happened to your mom."

Cynthia dabs a bit of the dark stain on the sock and onto the stair that is eye level to her.

"Which thing are we talking about here?" she asks with a

144

furrowed brow, "lotta things happened to my mom."

"The things that would concern the Dvorak Group directly."

"Which would be…"

"Apparently, we owned the factory where she got laid off. And the company that gave her the subprime loan for her house."

"Fuck's *sake*. Fuckin' one-percenters," she scoffed as she shook her head.

Ben chuckled as Cynthia continued to rub in a back and forth motion on the stairs. Suddenly she stops, examining the dark patch. She pops open another can.

"How would I even have known something like that?" Cynthia wonders aloud.

"I don't know."

"Well, that's one hell of a motive," she sighs, turning her sock to the opposite side and dipping it into the next can, "I suppose you could say I had the opportunity. Just had to convince you that I somehow had the means."

"Your first house. That you mentioned at dinner. That was what you did with the money?"

"Yes."

"Because you were homeless?"

Cynthia stops staining for a moment but then resumes, without looking up.

"Ancient history, but yes."

"While you were working downstairs?"

"Yes."

"The whole time?"

"Pretty much. What's with the interrogation?"

"Why wouldn't you tell me something so important?"

Cynthia furrows her brow again. "Didn't I?"

Ben scoffs. "Uh, no, Cynth, you didn't."

145

"You knew Mom and I had fallen on hard times."

"Yeah, I thought that meant you had to work to pay for culinary school, not that you didn't fucking have a home."

Cynthia shrugs. "It really wasn't all that bad. It got a little old. Winter time's a bitch, but... you know. We had a system. Never thought I'd say it, but Jersey's not a bad place to be homeless. Some days I kinda miss it."

"I must've sounded like an idiot."

"How so?"

"Droning on and on. About whatever 20-something yuppies drone on about. Grad school."

"Are you kidding? I loved being with you in the city. On-campus. I was totally swooning."

"Were you?" he grins.

"Um... yes," she says as though it were obvious. "You were this... hot, older boy. Rich. You had a car. I could give a *shit* about not having a house back then. Me playin' social. You jammin heavy den makin' a lime wit' ya *dougla* gyal. Likkle *jagabat*, eh?" Cynthia smiles, rubbing the stain into the stairs as though she's a million miles away. Ben has no idea what she's said, but it's probably as hot as it sounds.

"Never got to spend it on you."

"What, money? You lived in Soho, Ben. And you let me stay there rent-free."

"That's not what I mean, you know that."

"Yeah, well. You were still a 'scrub' at work, according to you. I definitely was."

"Is that why you took the money?"

"Honestly, Benji. It's done. I took the money and ran."

"It matters your circumstances," he says, defending her.

"There are plenty of people *with* homes who would've also

146

been happy to fuck off for 100 grand. Stop trying to make it virtuous."

Ben chuckles in amusement and frustration. "Who the hell downplays the fact that they were homeless?"

"I'm not downplaying anything. I'm telling you, it doesn't matter my circumstances, I made a choice."

"So you'd do the same thing again? Right now?"

"If I hadn't done it the first time, I wouldn't be here."

Ben toys with an empty gum wrapper in his hand. His security blanket for the moment. How long had he been fiddling with it? And where was the gum? He eyes the shiny paper, made dull with crumpling wrinkles.

"If it was a house you needed... I don't know why you wouldn't just tell me about it."

"Because you were my... I was your... girl... thing," Cynthia answers, returning the top to one can of stain, "and it was lovely, and surreal."

"As in 'not real.'"

"As in, I was young and irresponsible, and all I knew was that I didn't want it to end. And that would've ended it."

Ben doesn't move, trying not to show his satisfaction at her words. Does Cynthia know what she's confessing to him? She's all but revealing she was in love.

"You're wrong, by the way," he says.

"Really."

"What kind of guy do you think I was?"

"I don't fuckin' know, Ben. I was a homeless 20-year-old, trying desperately to keep my job while also fucking the heir apparent without getting in trouble. They'd warned us up and down about all of you, and there I was nodding my head like I was listening, trying to hide my morning dick breath," she went

147

on, smoothing in streaks of stain with her sock-covered hand.

"You had this whole thing about getting close to people and having them use you. 'Spoiling' people who were once genuine. You think I wasn't willing to *die* before I became one of those people to you? You obviously hated being associated with anything Dvorak at the time, so what was I gonna ask? I mean, honestly, it didn't really enter my mind. And yes, as in 'not real.' You had a fiancée!"

"Did *he* tell you that?"

"*You* certainly didn't."

"I'm not too sure how he found out about us, actually," Ben wondered.

"Probably by opening his eyes and looking."

"I wonder if he paid Doug, too."

"Benji, enough with your dad."

"Why are you *defending* him?"

"Do you think it's possible that maybe, for a split second, maybe your dad saw something in me?"

"I doubt it."

"That so," she gently retorts. Obviously wounded.

"That's not a reflection on you at all, I just mean... I'm sure he made you *think* he was being generous toward you, but you had something that he needed. You had more power than he let on."

"I know that you know your father in a way that I never could, but with all due respect Benji, you weren't in the room."

"I didn't need to be to know that he still got what he wanted. He drove us apart."

"He gave me an opportunity," Cynthia rebuts, shedding the sweat sock stained with Kona on one side and Mahogany on the other, "and I can't explain it, but I think he knew that I was going to do everything I could to make his investment worth it.

I think somehow he knew."

"...I'm glad my dad could give you everything you never had," Ben can't help sniping.

"He gave me the chance to never have to be manipulated by my circumstances ever again, and yeah, I'm grateful to him. Stop pretending like we had a chance, Ben," Cynthia reasons in a sympathetic voice.

"I was gonna propose. To you."

Cynthia doesn't stop her work at that piece of news. She's simply quiet as she sighs.

"Well. That would've been stupid," she finally says.

"You would've said 'no'?"

"Probably. Could've avoided this whole mess, now, couldn't we?"

"Why?"

"Because I was twenty!"

"I know that. We could've had a long engagement."

"Oh, *Lord.* Now I *know* I dodged a bullet."

The air becomes dead with silence. Ben feels her remorse, as well as his own wounded pride. He knows he deserves it.

He doesn't know how much longer he has before Cynthia will change the subject again. His closing window makes him brave.

"Did you really not know? How I felt?"

Cynthia scoffs a scoff of frustration. "I mean... I know we were making plans, but... marriage? I just remember feeling like you were trying to get rid of me. Like a pet your parents wouldn't allow you to have so you were just... hiding me in a shoebox."

"How could you say we didn't have a chance?"

"It was a Romeo and Juliet level clusterfuck, Ben."

"We have more of a chance now than most people. And we're practically strangers now."

149

Cynthia didn't know which part of that statement she objected to more.

"Is there a point to this?" Cynthia asks.

"No. I suppose... I'm just looking for answers."

"If you think after ten years, that I'm still the kind of girl that wants to follow around some indecisive workaholic, then you haven't been paying attention."

"Fair enough," Ben says, feeling like the challenger after the first round against the heavyweight champion. Beaten. Bloody. "So what's the timeline, Miss Gordon?"

"Everything's on schedule. Early even. The big reveal's next week."

"All this will be done by next week?"

"Miraculous, isn't it? Gabe and I will be there. I trust Esmee will want to see the finished product."

"Esmee?"

"Your fiancée."

"Yeah, I— I know who she is, I'm wondering why you think she would come."

"I... guess..." Cynthia begins before she just laughs and shakes her head. "Ay...yayay."

Her reaction makes Ben pause. She won't be there because she'll be gone. But Cynthia doesn't know that.

"You disapprove of our relationship?" he asks.

"To each his own, Benji."

"Give me your honest opinion, Cynth."

"Stop."

"I'm serious."

"Ben, don't think I don't know you're over there licking your wounds over the conversation we *just* had. I can't even share my opinion about *our* relationship without hurting your feelings."

"I want you to give me your most rawest, realest opinion of my impending marriage. I swear I will not get angry."

"Which stain do you like?" Cynthia suddenly asks.

He gives a sigh of indecision. "What's going on the walls?"

"White, more or less."

"This will be the trim as well?"

"Correct."

"The darkest one."

"Great choice."

"...Is this some kind of Yoda moment you're about to spring on me?"

Cynthia laughs as she hangs her head, her eyes sparkling like jewels and his heart skips a beat. It was the way she laughed when he told a bad joke. Or gave her a compliment out of the blue. Or unknowingly said what she was thinking.

"What can I say, Ben. You know me well."

"You're saying 'just fucking pick one?'"

"I'm saying... I understand the obsession with making the right choice. One you're gonna look at every day. Trust someone who has experience with staining. Not many people get a chance to buy more than one house, see more than one stain. I mean... you can re-stain shit, but you get where I'm going with this," Cynthia explains with her hands.

"They're all great. Melanie, me, Esmee, old whats-her-face from Brazil... you could be happy with anyone. Content, I should say. Once you make your decision, you'll give it everything you have to make it work. You're afraid to invest. You're used to everything being either a good deal or a bad deal."

Ben is having a hard time listening after hearing Cynthia put herself on this list.

"But this isn't like a money deal. It's like staining. Meaning, they're all great. Context matters, of course. Complimentary matches matter, of *course*, but... stain is beautiful. So beautiful in fact, that you can't make a wrong choice. So... pick the one that speaks to you, Ben."

* * *

Ben drives back into the city, distracted. He gets to the Dvorak group parking garage, to the top level just outside his office. He can't get out because he is sitting. Just sitting.

How could she say they didn't have a chance? Why would his father bother with breaking up something that didn't have a chance?

"You're wrong," he says to no one, an elbow propped across the steering wheel. He's never known Cynthia to be so wrong about him before. She was right about making things work, but he could never stomach a bad deal. And there was no worse deal than marrying the wrong woman. Even if he didn't marry for love, he couldn't.

She was also right that he needed to fuckin' pick already. It was the one area of life that he was ever indecisive.

His phone vibrates in his pocket at that precise moment.

Ben looks at it, expecting it to be from his assistant. But it isn't. It's a notification from Esmee's Instagram. She's taken a picture of herself in what looked to be a bridal veil with the caption, "window shopping at Kleinfeld's."

The emotional nausea he feels is suddenly overwhelming.

Fuck. *FUUUCK.*

Ben can no longer outrun the inevitable. He isn't going to marry this girl.

Eliminating choices is progress too, he supposes. But he

knows exactly what he has to do. Because when he thinks of having to break Esmee's heart, it feels like a walk in the park compared to what he's considering: picking the one that speaks to him.

Cynthia. It's the most obvious answer. She isn't with him, but she hasn't moved on. And so, neither could he. Even if he didn't marry her for love it just made sense. But he did love her. With a calm, steady love.

Perhaps he isn't indecisive at all. Perhaps he's just a moron. His gut instinct pulled him back from every fool marriage he tried to force. Every woman that succeeded in taking his mind off the woman he loves.

The thought of proposing to Cynthia causes his guts to churn and it puts a smile on his face. Jitters. His gut was going off like a metal detector over treasure.

He suddenly can't believe he has a chance to have what every man should. A woman to slay dragons for, the dragon being himself.

The only question is, could he survive her answer? He's spent the last ten years sheltering himself with ignorance. About what happened, why, and what to do about it. It is his personal jail of oblivion, where Cynthia could do no right or wrong, and as long as there were questions there was hope. He isn't sure if he knows how to be free of it.

Ben heads straight to Esmee's hotel, then to his penthouse apartment where Esmee is nowhere to be found. "*We need to talk. Tonight,*" Ben sends her a private message.

Maybe he's being rash, but the fact that Esmee is leaving for an untold number of weeks means that he has to do this now. This couldn't wait another long trip. It could barely wait another day.

He has to let go of Esmee. First. Or else he can never look Cynthia in the eye again. He has to go for broke.

After nearly an hour, Ben finds himself getting antsy, feeling the charlatan the longer he has to go without doing what he knows he has to.

"*Where are you?*" Ben sends her another message.

"*Out.*" is her reply after a ten-minute delay.

"*We need to talk.*"

"*Say what you have to say, Ben,*" is her unusually direct reply.

Ben sighs, feeling annoyed. Now's not the time to test his texting pet peeve.

"*I will not do this in a text,*" he sends back. Esmee responds with a flurry of texts that follow thusly:

"*Honestly, you millennials are snobs.*"

"*Technology is not inherently less legitimate.*"

"*For example, I know you probably think sending me a private message after my Kleinfeld's post was the proper thing to do, but you may as well have put it in the comments.*

"*It would've been better than not even LIKING my comment. After I fucking TAGGED YOU IN IT. It was FUCKING humiliating!*"

Ben tries to call her. Twice. But her phone instantly goes to voice mail, which means she's ignoring his calls. Instead, she sends another text.

"*Break up with me, Ben. Go on.*"

Since his apologetic tone can't be heard in a text, Ben crafts a message that he would never ever say if she was there in front of him. Angrily he presses send.

"*Honestly, Esmee, if I promised to help your brand after your modeling career is over, would you even mind?*"

It takes a few minutes before she responds and he's left to wonder her emotional state. But he struggles to feel sympathy.

Maybe next time she'll pick up the phone when he calls.

"You bastard," she finally answers.

"I said break up with me. Like a man. Own it."

"Yes, I mind. I mind that two years of my life have just gone to SHIT."

She's definitely crying right now. He can picture her shrill posh accent in his head. But it's nothing like the real thing. He still doesn't like texting, but he can see the allure.

"You're right," he concedes. *"I'm sorry."*

"I was going to marry you. I really was. I promise. I waited too late. Something in me kept tell me to wait."

"*telling."

Silence.

"It's Cynthia Gordon, isn't it?"

He can't tell if it's an angry question or not. In his head, her question is knowing and sympathetic.

"I don't even know if she will take me back. I don't think she will. She's already turned me down in a roundabout way. But I need to get down on both knees this time, hear the rejection from her and no one else. No presumptions."

"And if she says 'no'?"

"Then I'm fucked, I guess," Ben answers. He cringes, knowing she's thinking of taking sloppy seconds. He feels overwhelming guilt as he sends her a confirmation of his resolve.

"I can't marry you, Esmee. It would be so much less than you deserve, and you know it."

Still more silence.

"I begged you to be honest with me," she finally replies.

Ben sighs, answering.

"I know, I tried. I thought I was. But I wasn't being honest with myself, either.

"I'm not a liar, I'm just a moron."

"Fair enough," she answers. He doesn't know what to say back, if anything else even needs to be said. He starts a few messages but only ends up erasing them. In the interim, Esmee sends more texts.

"Were it anyone else I would've personally had you poisoned."

"You've never tried to hurt me, Ben. And I will always love you for that."

"Right then. I leave for Prague in two days. I will come for my things tomorrow. I would appreciate it if you weren't there."

Ben figures the best thing he could do is not patronize her, or send her off with false platitudes of affection. He sends her a curt response that is both a sword and a kindness.

"I won't be."

12

Ten Years Ago

I t was right before Thanksgiving that Cynthia met his girlfriend Melanie, when Ben brought her to work for a lunch date.

"So great to finally put a face to a name," Melanie smiled.

"Cynthia's going to house sit while we're in Aspen," Ben filled her in, casually.

"You're not going anywhere for the holidays?" Melanie frowned.

"Can't beat double time," Cynthia smiled sleepily.

"Double time, wow! Does Sol know his kitchen staff is getting that kind of money?"

"You know he does, Mel," Ben replied through gritted teeth.

Cynthia would've shaken her hand, but she was serving food to the two of them at the time. Her humiliation was so acute she was resolved to end it then and there, even though she had nowhere to go until next year when her mother's new apartment would finally be ready.

Ben obviously suspected as much. He slipped out when he knew Cynthia's shift was over and raced to his apartment, only to find she was in his room, instantly packing her things in a large duffle bag. She didn't acknowledge him when he came in.

"I'm sorry," he began.

Cynthia said nothing as she started emptying another drawer.

"Can you please stop doing that and talk to me?"

"Okay... what the hell were you thinking?"

"She said she wanted to meet you. I couldn't act like I had something to hide."

"Why would she even *want* to meet me?"

"Because she knows you're staying here. She'd be crazy not to."

"Well, she absolutely knows we're sleeping together."

"She doesn't. Trust me."

"I'm such an idiot for getting myself into this. This is going worse than nowhere."

"Don't say that."

"I won't say 'it's either me or her,' because I already know your choice. I can't believe you had me serving her food like a fucking—"

"Cynthia please, it's not like that, I'm sorry. And I promise I'll explain, and you can help me work this out I just... can we deal with this when I get back?"

Cynthia stopped, weeping threatening to overwhelm her. She was heartbroken and humiliated. But she was still a beggar, at least for the next few weeks.

Without having to worry about Cynthia, her mom had been able to save up first and last month's rent quickly and easily, and the apartment with the bonus room wouldn't be available until January. At the time, Cynthia urged her to wait for the bigger apartment but now, of course, she wished that she hadn't. She knew her mom probably suspected she was stalling in order to stay in the city with Ben.

She was a blind idiot. Time was never on her side. She kicked herself for ever letting herself get comfortable— with Ben, with anyone. As long as she didn't have a home, her dignity was always on the chopping block.

"I hate crying," she informed him.

"If you still want to end it after the holidays, it might kill me, but I'll understand. I don't say that to guilt you, I just... I hate that this happened, and if you leave right before I go on this trip, I will put a fucking gun in my mouth."

"You assume I don't want that to happen," Cynthia muttered. Ben relaxed. If she was making jokes, that meant there was hope.

"Don't you fucking dare," Cynthia sneered when he leaned in to kiss her, pulling away.

"Are you seriously going to work on Thanksgiving? While my father fucking skis and drinks butter rum?"

"I am. Your dad skis?"

"He does."

Ben sat down next to her on the floor against the edge of the bed. He was quiet for a moment, careful not to touch her like he instinctively wanted while he continued.

"It's perfectly okay with me if you still hate me after today, and I have no right to ask you for a single thing, I know that. But if you never do another thing for me, do this one thing out of the goodness of your heart, which I know is there, because it's why I love you."

He used the "L" word but he'd say anything at this point, she told herself cynically. A bundle of tears fell from her cheeks.

"Please, please, please just be here when I get back. Please."

"Sounds like you're begging," she said, wiping her face.

"I am," Ben said, his hands aching to wipe her tears and console her.

Needless to say, Cynthia took him back. Hearing him come through the door after two weeks of radio silence practically unraveled her. She was doomed and she knew it.

There are worse things to be addicted to while homeless, she said to herself, as Ben abandoned his luggage at the door and made a beeline straight to where she was on the couch.

Sex. It completely changed their relationship. From the moment Cynthia kissed him he knew there was no going back, and it never seemed to be enough. Beyond arousal, Ben felt out of body whenever Cynthia undressed in front of him. The first time she showed him all of her, part of him wanted to look away because he didn't deserve it.

Their lovemaking was quiet in nature, which surprised Ben pleasantly. He always loved Melanie's theatrics and thought he was officially converted after her. In college, the thought of her screaming his name throughout the day would get him so rock hard he couldn't wait to track her down between classes, peel her away from whatever study group she was at, and rush her back to his dorm.

But after the first time he'd made love to Cynthia, he'd started to worry that most, if not all of it, was fucking fake. And after their two week holiday in Aspen, he had his answer.

He tried to just let Cynthia sleep when he got home in the evenings. He only had so many hours to sleep himself with his schedule. But he always ended up waking her with his touch, his mouth on her smooth, tight skin until one of those precious moans escaped her throat and he had to find her hips with hands and grip them tightly, so tight until he could completely lose himself in her and be satisfied, if only until their bodies would meet again.

On this particular morning, Cynthia was the one to wake him. She took him into her mouth while he was still asleep, and for a moment he fought waking because he thought the feeling was coming from his dream. He awoke to the sight and sounds of her head bobbing up and down his lap, the bright pink tips of her hair brushing across his bare chest. He let her continue until he thought he would die if he wasn't inside her.

"Get on top. Hurry," he instructed her urgently.

Cynthia liked being on top. Ben liked being torn between the sight of her body and gazing into those translucent eyes of hers. She hastily got in position, grabbed his manhood and slowly slipped it inside. He held his breath, afraid he would miss her initial reactions to his needy thrusts.

Finally, his lungs were bursting, his heart beating so fast it felt like he could never get enough oxygen. He wasn't going to last very long. He grabbed at her t-shirt and methodically she shed it, knowing what he was after. He wanted to come while watching her tits bounce, a look of gorgeous anguish blooming across her face. He hiked up one of her legs, found the spot that she liked, and went to town. He watched her hand go between her legs and it was the last thing he saw before climax took over and he thrashed underneath her, his large hands and her narrow hips practically fused together.

His eyes were still closed as he noticed he was slick with sweat, her hot humid breath hitting his earlobe as their panting subsided. He slowly became aware of the frantic sounds of the city from the open windows. A breeze far too mild for December crept through the windows.

"What was that for?" he breathed.

"It's an unseasonably warm day and I'm happy," Cynthia

161

cooed. She planted a kiss on his lips and smiled as she rolled next to him.

"Why, because you're really a mermaid?"

"What?"

"Nothing," he said. "That's what you do when you're happy?"

"Isn't that what everyone does?"

"No," he chuckled.

"Kiss me," she replied. He rolled to his side and loomed over her, complying with a kiss on her temple.

"Do you know your mom's schedule?" he suddenly asked.

"Sure. Why?"

"I want to take her to dinner."

"My mom?"

"She's from Grenada, right?"

"Right."

"I found a Grenadian restaurant."

"You what?"

"I found a Grenadian restaurant in the city."

Cynthia just looked dumbfounded in response.

"You think your mom would like that?"

"I think... she would probably cry. Especially if they do it wrong. But I can't imagine a Grenadian restaurant existing at all if they were going to do that. Do they serve oil down?"

"What's that?"

"It's like, the national dish. It has a thousand ingredients and takes a thousand years to make."

"I don't know but I can find out."

"Why do you want to take my mom out?"

"Why not? A friend of mine mentioned a Grenadian restaurant and my ears perked up. I think she would get a kick out of it. She's such a nice lady. For, you know, letting me schtup you."

Cynthia smiled. "Alright."

"Give me a date and we'll go."

"You sure you'll have time? To go to dinner?"

"I'll make time."

"I think we're being followed. Have you noticed?" Cynthia asked.

Ben felt a bit embarrassed. "I noticed."

"Is that... normal?"

"Our dad always kept tabs on us when he could. But recon work is a new level. For me. I don't remember him much caring what I did. He followed my older brother all the time."

"Jesus. Why?"

"I don't know. Usually, my brother stopped whatever he was doing not long after."

"Oh no, Benji."

"But my brother was... special. And it never was over a relationship."

Cynthia rolled herself into his arms. "Did I do something to tip them off?"

"I think we both did."

"We hardly see each other at work."

"That's the point. We went from chatting it up to chatting it up a little too much, to nothing."

Cynthia smiled. "They're onto us. What do we do?"

"I have an idea, but it's flimsy."

"I'm all ears."

"I can put out a rumor that we dated, but then we broke up. Just among the guys. So that stupid plant Leland can send it back to my dad. It might require some... acting. And we may have to stop seeing each other for a while. A week or two should do it."

Cynthia's energy shifted against her will. It would still be another month until she and Bev had a place of their own.

She didn't plan on having to keep her homelessness a secret. They weren't even still supposed to be homeless by now. It was supposed to be a bump in the road.

She could just tell him the truth. But she would then become like most of the people in his life, and she didn't want to see the change in him once he realized she had no real place to go. She didn't want their relationship to be tainted by it at all. God, she fucking hated it. At times she nearly forgot, until they had conversations like this.

She didn't expect this thing with Ben to last, and she wasn't quite sure why. Other than the fact that life just didn't let good things last for long, especially if they were rooted in secrets and lies.

"It'll be hard, I know," he smiled, trying to read her mind. "I've gotten used to waking up to you."

"What about Melanie?"

"What about her?"

"What if she finds out?"

"I honestly don't care anymore. She's literally not even listening to me at this point."

"Where am I supposed to go for a week or two?"

Ben put the obvious out of his mind. She felt left in limbo. As did he. Though he doubted that Cynthia felt as nauseous as he did about his cowardly indecision.

He simply couldn't have broken it off with Melanie during the holidays. It wouldn't even be taken as anything but a joke. Plus, if he were to burn virtually all of his bridges, he needed to come up with a plan. And with his father closing in, playtime with Cynthia was truly over. It was time to get his future figured out.

If Cynthia didn't want to— or couldn't— go home, then he

should man up. She was just starting to leave things at his place. Starting to feel comfortable.

"I can put you up someplace close. Someplace nice."

Cynthia's energy continued to plummet. What could he say to stop it? He cursed to himself. He saw his life in a different light looking at Cynthia's face, suddenly like a scared animal.

"And if they find out about us? What happens then?"

"Then... I don't know, I'll cross that bridge when we get to it. It's not like he could ever stop me from seeing you."

"Are you ever going to tell Melanie the truth?"

"Obviously I am. Obviously, I have to."

Cynthia was quiet again and Ben could sense her dismay. Her uncertainty. He didn't know how, but one day this part of their lives would be a distant, dwarfed memory they could laugh about.

Suddenly he saw a flash of the future. Cynthia an award-winning chef. He, her financial tycoon husband. Treating clients to dinner at her very own restaurant in the city. The vision gave him a jolt of elation, followed by anxiety and anguish, dense like a pit in the center of a fruit.

Would he be able to let her go? To all the places she needed to go, to become that woman?

The answer was yes.

"If I paid for your culinary schooling, would you go?"

"What?"

"If I paid for it. For you to go to the finest school. In Paris. Would you go?"

Cynthia shifted.

"The finest school is here in New York."

"You didn't even look outside of the U.S. I know that you didn't."

"Where would you get that kind of money? Without anyone knowing?"

"It wouldn't have to be a secret. Hell, I could probably get my dad to pay for it if it meant you moving 1,000 miles away."

A thousand miles away.

"I can't leave my mom. I can't leave you."

"Cynthia, you can't sit in this apartment, waiting for me to come home, wasting your life—"

"I'm not wasting my life. I'm working, I'm saving up money—"

"For what?"

Cynthia was so close to just blurting it all out. But she was growing more concerned that he seemed so eager to get rid of her. And then... did she even want to be in food service for the rest of her life?

"Isn't that what you wanted? Didn't you beg me to be here when you got home?" asked Cynthia defensively.

"I did. And I'm grateful for that."

"So why do you want to get rid of me?"

"Cynth, you know that's not—"

"Get rid of your girlfriend. That you don't love. Why am I disposable? Because I don't have money?"

"What? No. Because I have to finish school, I have to take over The Dvorak Group, and to do that, I have to work my ass off."

"And you don't have time to babysit me."

He sighed.

"Don't think I don't want to keep coming home to you every day, because I do. But it's selfish. You're talented, you're hardworking. The world needs your chicken fried steak and your butter chicken, and... whatever else you come up with."

"So we're breaking up."

He smiled at her reasoning. They never settled on exactly what they were, but there wasn't a more appropriate term for what being apart from each other would be. He cradled her face in his hand.

"No. We're making a plan. For the future. I didn't say today. In fact, let's not talk about it now. Tell your mom about dinner. Okay?"

"Fine."

"I'm inviting my sister. She's basically my closest friend. Besides you. Do you know what that means?"

"What?"

"It means that I'm serious about this. I'm gonna do right by you, Cynth. It's just... people have been manipulating me my entire life. Trying to get me to do what's best for them and get me to go along with it. Instead of just telling me what they want and letting me decide. This isn't just which college to go to, this is an entire reality I'm altering. I gotta out-think these fuckers, Cynthia."

"Ben... wouldn't it be simpler to just... walk away? Give it all up? Like you said your brother did?"

"No."

"Why?"

"Because *fuck* Solomon Dvorak. I've worked too hard."

"Benji—"

"There's a way to have it all, Cynth. There is. And I'm gonna figure it out."

* * *

"How is it, mom?"

Cynthia, Ben and his sister Valerie all looked at Bev with bated

167

breath, as she tried the oil down from Mooma's, the Grenadian restaurant Ben took them all to.

The cook and the waiter too looked on from their stations. Within three chews she was giving them the "ok" sign, making them smile.

"See!" the cook exclaimed, his dark skin making his white smile practically glow. "Allyuh hungry awah?"

"I could tell from deh smells it was gonna be right, enuh," she smiled, savoring the brothy stew. They brought the entire stew pot to the table.

"This is *insane*," Ben remarked when he took a bite. Val nodded with her mouth full.

Even Cynthia had to look on with fascination as she watched her mother go full patois with the restaurant staff, looking like Indian Claire Huxtable. Only Cynthia had the vaguest idea what they were saying, but they all knew when something funny was being said.

"Boy, yuh is a pappy*show*!" Bev exclaimed to the cook.

"What just happened, Cynth?" Ben would chuckle.

"It's not as funny as it sounds," Cynthia replied with a laugh.

They politely asked Bev more and more about herself, which she artfully dodged in true Gordon fashion, volleying the questions back to Ben and his sister.

"So tell me. Yuh born walking dat way Benji, awat?"

"No. Actually, I couldn't walk at all until I was ten."

"My faddah's first baby, he lost. My half sistah. She couldn't move her left side at all, t'was so stiff. Couldn't control heh *tongue*."

"That sounds like Ataxic Cerebral Palsy. That's kind of rare. Mine is the common type, which is Spastic CP. There's some part of my brain that didn't get oxygen when I was in utero, and the muscles in my legs don't get sent certain signals. The walk comes from my other muscles overcompensating for the weak ones."

"Does it hurt, enuh?"

"Sometimes, yeah. Can't stand up for too long."

"Yuh ever wish yuh walked normal-like?"

"Mom..." Cynthia quietly nudged her.

"What? Deh man's grown. He knows I doh mean no disre-spect."

"They told me I never would, so I'm happy to be walking at all."

"It's all yuh know, ent it?"

"Yeah 'mon," Ben replied, which earned him a hit across the chest from Cynthia.

"You didn't tell Cynthia about the surgery?" Val wondered.

"No, I did not."

"What surgery?"

"Melanie recommended it," Valerie piped up. Cynthia's heart revved with shame and guilt. Ben hit Val hard underneath the table.

"Who's Melanie?" Bev asked harmlessly.

"Family friend," Val tried to recover.

"Apparently there's a procedure they could do that would cause the muscles in my legs to relax and give me a much more... 'normal' gait." Ben filled her in.

"They use *botox*, isn't that fascinating?" Val marveled.

"Well, now!"

"Are you thinking about doing it?"

"Sort of. Not really," Ben waffled. "I promised myself no more surgeries."

"This one would be nothing like the others. It's basically outpatient," Val pushed.

"Had a pretty bad panic attack before the last one."

"But you were like, ten."

"Yeah, so it was extra brutal. I'd only be doing it for someone else at this point."

"You know I looked into having their licenses removed. Suing the hospital," Val carried on their increasingly private conversation.

"Dr. West is no longer practicing," Ben said as though it were good news.

"I heard. Don't think *that* was a coincidence."

"Wait, what happened when you were ten?" Cynthia asked.

"Nothing that we can prove."

"Ben suspects that not every surgery that he had was... necessary."

"Holy *shit*."

"Our mother was obsessed with him being 'a cripple' as she called it. I think she liked the attention. She did everything the doctors told her, and Dad did everything our mother told him."

"I didn't suspect anything until the fourth surgery. One of my therapists up and quit, she was so upset."

"How have you not sued them?"

"Believe me, if we could get our dad to believe us, it would be total scorched Earth."

"But that would involve him entertaining the idea that he was outsmarted."

"Dat's awful Benji."

"It is, so let's change the subject."

"Okay, Benji. What yuh makin' a lime wit' an ol' woman for? Yuh plan t'marry my Cynt'ya awat?"

Ben didn't understand much of the question besides the

last part. Cynthia's instant reddening face let him know he understood it well enough. He answered by grinning over at Cynthia, grabbing her hand and kissing it.

Cynthia looked back at him, feeling dread. Knowing that once her mother got the apartment, she was going to have to find the courage to break it off, since he couldn't. He was going to be the next CEO of the Dvorak Group, and she had to find that next thing she was going to be— whatever that is.

Serving him lunch would be hella awkward after that. But she knew him. He wanted her, but he also wanted the best for her. He'll understand and get over it, eventually.

Maybe she'll take him up on that culinary school offer. But no way was she going to France. Unless he was willing to pay for her mom to go too. All the recipes were hers, after all.

She smiled at Ben's reaction to her mother's nosy question before rolling her eyes, cynically.

"*Doh beat up*, Mom," Cynthia shook her head, her mouth full of Grenadian food.

13

Present Day

C ynthia pulls up to the newly completed house boasting the tin roof, bold turquoise door, stately white porch columns and wood-stained shutters. She's dressed in a casually elegant black dress that fans out at the waist, simple matching flats on her feet. A single gold watch adorned her wrist and her hair is pinned back in a high demure ponytail. She notices the address numbers she ordered for the side of the door came in at some point, and her crew knew what she wanted.

The Moss property is officially done. The client reveal is tomorrow afternoon, and Cynthia commences her private design property walkthrough alone, her professional tradition.

She brings her box of personal touches, heavier and heavier with each new project. She fluffs pillows, she puts prop 1st editions on selective shelves and fireplace mantles, she examines the grout lines. She eyes the cut of the marble until her blurring vision plays tricks on her. She really did have the best people working for her. It was time to talk raises.

This is her ritual, the moment she lives for. When all the screaming panic she starts with has been completely vanquished by her fully realized vision: the aspirations, the mishaps, the delays, and the serendipitous moments all coming together to create something valuable. The intangible becomes real and far bigger than her.

This was her biggest challenge to date. The unlimited budget nearly killed her. But she slew the giant. It is more than she could've asked for. She's outdone herself. Not that he even cares, but Ben is going to be very happy. Or at least, impressed.

By the time she gets to the master bedroom, she's usually crying. The master is the room she always spends the most money on.

It's supposed to be a haven. Her mother always treated her bedroom that way. Especially in the house she grew up in, the one they lost. They never had much, but her mother's bedroom was always bedecked with photos and fabrics, laces, and pillows. The most beautiful patterned bedspreads that nourished the eye. Best of all, Cynthia was always allowed in.

She puts the same energy into all her master bedrooms. She's convinced it's what sells a house every time.

She retreats to the upstairs hallway bathroom a blubbering mess, thankful she stages every home with a realistic supply of toiletries to make buyers feel they're at home already. She steals a glance at the extra-large marble shower with a bench that spans the length of it. Like the locker room showers at the rec center. She always loved the look and spirit of that design and wanted to see it done in a home. She couldn't stop staring and she knew she'd found a new design element to get stuck on for the next five years.

"I outdid myself this time, Mama," she says as she takes a few sheets of soft toilet paper from the silver stand in the bathroom. She gives herself a few blinks in the quaint oval mirror before turning off the light and heading back downstairs.

"You were right. The stairs look stunning."

Cynthia startles at the sound of Ben's voice at the bottom of the stairs.

Making her way down, she is greeted by the sight of Ben at the front of the banister holding a bottle of wine. She stops in her tracks.

"You actually used the stain I picked out."

"I meant what I said, they're all beautiful. What are you doing here?" she rasps, her fist full of tissue paper.

"Is this a bad time?"

"You're not supposed to be here until the big reveal tomorrow."

"I'd much rather have you show me around. Never been big on crowds."

"...The three of us is a crowd?"

"You know what I mean."

She sniffs as she shakes her head, rolling her eyes as she touches the bridge of her nose.

"Why did I ever think you were taking this project seriously, to begin with?"

"I do take it seriously."

"You bought this house to keep me under your thumb, Ben."

"Not true."

"Then what?"

"It was an investment."

"That you stole from under me."

"Pardon me for wanting to throw some business your way."

Cynthia could only laugh. "You're insane, you know that?"

"Anyway, I didn't come here to fight. I brought wine so we could toast our successful business venture, and I'd like the tour.

If you don't mind."

Cynthia shrugs with a sigh of resignation.

"You're the boss," she replies with a lazy blink of her eyes.

She took him on the mostly wordless tour that started in the newly imagined kitchen.

"Wow."

"You like it?" she grins, trying to dodge his penetrating gaze.

"It's like night and day," is his unsatisfying response. "You put the elevator in," he also says. Yet another gloriously factual statement.

"I did."

"Why?" he smiled.

"I couldn't just tear out the laundry chute and drywall it up. I had to repurpose it. And I had an unlimited budget."

He tossed his head this way and that. "Kind of a useless extravagance."

"Not really," she defended, "Families with small children. Elderly parents who want the upstairs master. There's plenty of possibilities."

She watches as he takes everything in, seeing if he would give anything away in his eyes that he was impressed. He didn't.

The tour ends in the backyard that is now vivid green and fenced in tall, rich-colored cedar. They sit on the luxurious cushions of the sectional patio couch she'd picked out, the rectangular stone fire pit ablaze and filled with glass pebbles as they stretched out in front of it. They open the wine and retrieve two glasses from the outdoor bar area on the deck overlooking the woods behind the house. Cynthia looks over at Ben while he pops the cork of the expensive bottle of white. He has dressed in yet another crisp white shirt and dark chocolate slacks, more dressy than business.

"Did you leave a soirée to come here?"

"Something like that."

"How'd you know I'd even be here right now?"

"Your assistant told me where you were."

"I think she has a bit of a crush on you."

"She told me."

Cynthia huffed a laugh.

"Why were you crying?" he asked.

"When?"

"Earlier. When I came in I heard you crying."

She shrugged a bit with a nervous snicker. "It's come to be a ritual. Final day always gets me emotional. I put my all into it, and then I give it away. It's like giving away your baby."

"You make it sound draining."

"It is."

"Why do you do it?"

Cynthia shrugs. "It's the way I've always done it. Seems to be what works."

He chuckles softly, reminiscing. "First time I went to my Junior VP's house, I swear I could feel you. It was the strangest thing."

"I lived for that fucking bathroom," she remembers.

"The bamboo countertops."

"Right?"

"Very bold choice."

"If I didn't know better, Benji, I'd say you had an eye for design, too."

"For beauty, perhaps," he says, shedding a rare nervous grin as he looked down into his wine glass. Cynthia held back her own grin as she eyed him.

"You haven't told me what you think, yet."

"About?"

She gave him an amused, reprimanding look.

"Of your 'investment,'" she clarified.

"You care about what I think?"

"Of course, I designed it with you in mind."

"Why?"

"What do you mean why," she chuckles, "it's your house."

"But I'm selling it. This was supposed to be *your* vision."

"Yes, but it's my vision for *your* house. I tried to capture certain things about you that... I liked. That you used to like."

"Things you miss?"

"...Okay. Yes. Things I miss."

The silence lingers as Cynthia swishes wine around in her glass. He should propose to her right here and now. But he has no ring. He can't bear to do a single other half-assed thing regarding Cynthia.

"It reminds me of you, the house. The transformation. Not that you were a scary wreck that smelled like cat-piss before, but... you get what I mean."

"No, I don't, Ben," she egged him on with a grin.

"Everything that was beautiful about the house then is beautiful about it now. No matter if it's glamorously made over or smells like old grease, and wears ugly, oversized chef's uniforms. That's what I mean."

Cynthia's heart aches as she looks at Ben, the one stupid thing in her life that she childishly whines about not being able to have, to this day. Life has been so uncommonly hard.

She just wants him, and it's not fair. *It's not fair.* She's about to say the words aloud.

"Maybe I should keep it," he suddenly says. It snaps Cynthia out of her trance.

177

"The house, you mean?"

"Yes."

For some reason, her pulse skyrockets.

"...Ben, don't be silly," Cynthia scoffs.

"You really want me to sell this house?"

"Of course."

"To the highest bidder?"

"That's... usually how it works."

"I think I want to keep it. In fact, I think I want *you* to have it."

"What? No, Ben. It goes on the market."

"Your very heart and soul is in every detail of this house."

"Yes. And my heart and soul is what sells."

"Well, enough selling. I doubt I'll make very much money on it anyway. You pulled out all the stops, and I'm glad to see what my unlimited budget could do. I'm honored. And I want you to have it. It's time you enjoyed your own hard work."

"Says the man who inherited everything he has."

Ben takes the bottle and refills his wine glass with a sigh.

"Cynth, enough. You're constantly taking swipes at me."

"Me? You talk like someone who owns the world, and frankly it's annoying."

"You're also well-to-do now, Cynthia. You sacrificed everything to get here, I should think you would enjoy it more."

"Being your side piece for six months is hardly 'everything.'"

Her words are meant to wound him and they succeed.

"I'm trying to do something nice for you."

"And I appreciate the gesture, but I don't want it done."

"You're just going to keep giving away the best parts of you? Just because someone's willing to give you some cash?"

"Frankly, yes. Because some people didn't grow up affording

178

everything."

"Oh, for fuck's sake."

"Those people have to give over very large sums of money. They have to go into debt for decades, and in exchange, they get something very very beautiful, a personal piece of art they get to live in."

"I'm familiar with the process."

"You should be. You literally export it."

"Don't you want to feel what they feel? For longer than a few months?"

"I can't feel what they feel, Benji. It's not the same. I have to give it away."

"It sounds like you're refusing to be happy."

"No."

"No?"

"It makes me happy to be valued, to have a vision and then see it carried out. Not to live in a *shrine* I created to myself."

"A shrine you created to yourself? Or to us?"

Cynthia's silent, stewing, as if to deny that he's sitting right there next to her. Whether she's snapped into a trance or out of one, he can't quite discern. Either way, he senses the subject is wildly tender.

"Is that it? Is this... our house, Cynth?"

The notion is adorable, almost childlike. Not almost, it is. And he is completely taken aback. *That little liar*, he thinks.

"That's why you put in the elevator? Is it for me?"

"Don't flatter yourself," she snipes curtly. She picks up the wine bottle from the table and tops off her glass. "You didn't know whether you would buy or sell. I figured you would change your mind again at the last minute, and I was right. Rich types like you are always doing that. You had an unlimited budget."

But her words at face value suddenly sound ridiculous to him. He can't believe he'd ever allowed his insecurities to overpower the obvious truth.

Suddenly he understands. This moment only makes sense with all the others if she really loved him. Loves him.

"Is that why you don't want to live in it?" he deduces.

"Of course I don't want to *live* in it!" Cynthia cries.

It's all she says before she looks away with a scoff, and for a moment Ben wonders if she might just get up and go home. She sits there with her wine, sipping it absent-mindedly instead.

After a long silence, she begins again, matter-of-factly and with a far off look.

"The house. The one that we lost all those years ago. It had a carport. And this... kickass basement. It wasn't really a basement, just a lower level. It had its own entrance. It was gonna be my apartment when I graduated. I was gonna pay rent."

"Cynthia..."

"I just wanted to picture it. I just wanted to picture it, and then give it away. And then *you* called... out of the blue. You stole it from under me, and you just... fucked it all up. And you obviously had money to burn. I kept trying to think bigger and bigger and bigger..."

She takes a sip of her wine. A big one. They're both silent until finally, Cynthia has to speak. His stare is unnerving.

"It doesn't mean anything, alright? My mind, it just grabs hold of something... we were just two dumb kids, I know that—"

Ben silences her with a hand on her lips. Cynthia recoils.

"*Don't*... fucking play me, Ben."

"I'm not. I would never."

"All you've ever done was play me," she spits, her eyes turning steely.

As Cynthia brings up the past without his prompting, Ben senses a breakthrough. He puts down his wine glass and moves in close, as if coaxing someone off a ledge.

"I never... lied to you, Cynthia. I wouldn't. I was young. I'd never lost anything and I fucked up. I fucked up bad. But I never lied. You have to believe me," he responds, pleading vulnerability in his eyes.

Cynthia breathes hard as she looks at him, as he's letting her probe him. He barely blinks, daring her to doubt him. Her eyes dart back and forth as she soaks him in again, until she sees the boy that used to hold up the chow line and it makes her shake.

"It doesn't mean anything," she insists, breathless. "I hardly even knew what I was doing."

"It's beautiful. You're beautiful," he says. He grabs her hand and she tries to hide how much it startles her as she looks down at it. Have they touched before now?

"What are you doing?"

"I'm choosing, Cynth. I choose you. It's you. It's always been you."

"I don't understand—"

"I broke it off with Esmee."

"You... what?! When?"

"Right after we talked. Right after you told me you were beautiful like stain and I could be happy with you. You were right about everything except one thing. I can't be with just anyone. It has to be you. I want you to have this house, and I want you to live in it. With me."

"Benji!"

"I thought I had time to do right by you. Back then. I knew I didn't have forever but... I thought I had time. To have it all.

181

And I *lost* you," Ben lets out in a gruff whisper, a reflecting pool of emotion collecting in his eyes. "And now it's ten years later, and I damn near made the same mistake again. I'd love to tell you that this was my plan all along, to give you everything you ever wanted and deserved, but it wasn't my plan. At all. It's *better* than my plan. Marry me, Cynth. Live here. With me. In our house and choose me back. *Please*."

Cynthia freezes, stunned.

"Unbelievable," she shakes her head, leaning forward and slowly setting her goblet down on the glass coffee table in front of them.

"You're crazy. Crazy and spoiled, Ben, you know that?"

He does know that. He says nothing, only follows her brazen movements as she turns back to face him on the couch, eyeing his lips and he knows exactly what is happening.

Gently he grabs her face in his hands as she grabs his. Their lips crash together.

Now that he's kissing her for the first time in ten years, it seems obvious.

"Cynthia," he chants, remorse, of all things, washing over him. "I'm so sorry."

"Just shut up," she whispered, emotion in her voice. She kisses him as though it were a compulsion, with no end in sight. Some fast, some slow and deep. She doesn't let a nanosecond go by without another.

This. This is what had been missing, he realizes, as he lets her take her fill. This is what he wanted to say to her, despite his regret. And despite her anger she'd wanted to say it back. This whole time.

He lets Cynthia straddle him as he holds her waist, with his arm so tight around her that she gasps. Tears pour out of her eyes as though he's physically squeezed emotions out of her. His mouth engulfs hers again and he can feel her body tense frantically, rocking him forward. Her lips break from his as she throws her arms around his neck and clings to him, sobbing. He pulls her towards him, holding her as if they were on the edge of a cliff.

He tries to hide the fact that he's rock hard within seconds of this heartfelt moment. But he can't. And the moment Cynthia can feel him, her body is grinding against his and clinging to his rod like a magnet. She pulls forcefully away from him to undo the buttons on her dress so she can peel down the top of it.

He wants to undo his pants and free his cock but he doesn't want to be presumptuous, even though he can read Cynthia's sparkling eyes and thoughts now the way he used to. Sure enough, her hands go to his belt buckle and he takes over the job, leaving her to undo her nude-colored bra.

"*Fuck*," he exclaims at the sight of a topless Cynthia, the rushing sensation of her hand around his cock again for the first time in ten years. His voice echoes in the private darkness of the narrow back patio, lined by the tall cedar fence and greenery.

He breathes in frustration. He wants her too much. But she needs this, and he can't let her down.

Once she lowers herself onto him, their calm, quiet chemistry once again takes over as though their first time were yesterday. Ben closes his eyes tight, trying to shield himself from the image of Cynthia's ecstasy so he can last as long as possible. He digs his fingertips into her thighs. Her breath hits his ear again and again as she tightly clings to him, her gasps turning to sobs that Ben can't decipher. Whether they're happy sobs or not, his heart breaks for his Cynthia, whom he inadvertently left out in the cold and still took him back without warning.

"Don't stop," she weeps.

"Oh, Cynth," he quietly moans, taking her face into his hands, distracting himself with her kiss until he can regain his composure enough to resume his steady strokes, deeper this time.

"*Oh my God*," Cynthia groans and grits her teeth. Sex with Ben is as good as it ever got for her. She never felt so loved and adored. Practically worshipped. And it only seemed to feel like anything when those brown eyes were looking back at her, his smooth, firm hands touching her. She regrets taking it for granted.

"*Fuck!* Benji!"

He slinks one arm around her waist and holds her even tighter against him with the other, his composure unraveling.

"I'm gonna fuckin' come inside you, baby," he whispers, a filthy lament.

"Yes!" she whispers.

Fuck. Cynthia Gordon is once again calling his name, begging him to breed her like a beautiful dream. He let her do it a lot more than he should have in the past, because in the moment he simply could not give a fuck. It became his way of forcing fate's hand, making it easier to break off the engagement if Cynthia turned up pregnant.

He questioned her motives after that, but now she is once again letting him fill her, which means she's still that same wild girl, making her way around the world on just her instincts. And she finds him worthy. Still.

"I need to hear you say it again."

"Come inside me, Benji."

"That's what you want?"

"That's what I want."

"Say it fucking loud."

She says it again and again, completely out of her mind until she is emptying her muffled cries over and over into his shoulder as she milks his cock with her hips, chasing her release that comes with a vengeance on the heels of his own. It is a noise record for the couple, and Cynthia is a sobbing mess by the end. He continues to hold her as they breathe hard. He can tell by the rasp in her voice that she's emotional, much more than he is, and he could kick himself for being so blind, so self-absorbed.

"I love you so much," Ben whispers. Cynthia responds with a kiss on his neck. She raises her lips to his ear.

"My mama's gone," she confides.

He smoothes her hair with a heavy sigh. "I know," he whispers gently.

"She didn't even get to see..."

"I'm so sorry, Cynth."

"That *fucking* money," she pants, forlorn. She rocks on him a bit as if in tangible pain, beating a clenched hand against him. Ben's chest tightens.

"That's *not* what did it," he sternly insists, "That's not your fault."

"She was fine when we lived in the van," she meekly protests.

"Cynthia, stop it. You're driving yourself insane."

"God wouldn't take her if we were still on the street, because I needed her," she confesses the rest of her paranoid delusion. "I buried her here because I didn't want to be alone. She should be buried next to Daddy, but I couldn't..."

Ben just cradles her head nestled in the crook of his neck as she continues to sob relentlessly. Finally, limp with exhaustion, her head still resting on his shoulder, she whispers, "please don't hate me," her head rocking back and forth pitifully.

"I could never, ever hate you, Cynth. Do you hear me?"

"Promise me you won't," she raises her head and looks at him intently.

"Cynthia... I promise," he says, wiping her tears with his thumbs. He grabs her raw face and kisses her again, this time slow and needy, until she's reaching between his legs again. His mind races at the thought of Cynthia's insatiable need for him and his body responds in kind, another record..

"Cynthia, wait—"

"Don't tell me no, Ben," she moans.

"I won't, but... not here. Not like this."

"Yes, here. Yes like this."

"Why?"

"Because we can. Because it's your house. Our house."

"I've waited ten years—"

"I *know*."

"I want to make love, Cynthia."

Cynthia whined, laying her head on his shoulder. She was never very good with waiting. He chuckled, his new reality still feeling new and dreamy.

"Let's take a shower. Like we used to?"

"Did you notice the bench?" she sniffs.

"In the upstairs master? I did," he smiled, "let's try it out."

Wordlessly they retreat upstairs, entering the cavernous bathroom with the long shower bench. Cynthia leans against the double vanity with a flirty smile.

"Age before beauty," she says. Ben starts to strip unceremoniously, loosening, unhooking and unbuttoning from head to toe until peeling it all off was the only job left.

"Do you think our neighbors heard all that?" Ben asks as he watches Cynthia reach for her own buttons on her black dress.

186

"Probably."

"That might be a new public record."

"Lotta records broken tonight," she smirked as she began to pull her dress over her head. Ben stops her, undressing her himself. Cynthia undresses him back until they're both naked.

They try not to ogle each other until they are both wet, until the temperature was just right and they were shrouded underneath a canopy of white noise, the sound of pressured water all around them. The sight of Cynthia's naked form is instantly arousing and Ben doesn't hide his enthusiasm. Heat and emotion mingle together in his big brown adoring gaze and Cynthia is melting all over again, feeling his broad, sinewy bare shoulders for the first time in a decade. When their lips finally meet again, soft and wet with tears and tongues and the heat of the shower, they find their words once again, kissing and caressing apologies. Panting and moaning regret. Groping promises to never let go again.

They reunite in the California king of the master bedroom, where Ben takes his time driving Cynthia back and forth to the brink, slowly making love to her until they are again spent.

"I guess I can cancel the reveal tomorrow," Cynthia lazily replies with her eyes closed.

"Don't. It's important to you."

"Not if we already used the shower. And the bed."

"And the patio," he smirks, stroking her hair, her head on his chest.

"Did you really break it off with Esmee?"

"Of course."

"Don't say it like that, like I'm crazy. You have a history of leaving fiancées in the wind."

"I have done *some* growing in ten years, Cynth."

187

"I'll say," she said with a naughty grin that had his cock stirring. "How'd she take it?"

"Better than I expected. She seemed to know it was coming."

"Where's she now?"

"Probably landed in Prague this morning."

"I hope she's okay. I liked her, Benji."

"Me too. She reminded me of you. A lot. I didn't know that, at the time."

"...I don't know if we should've done this."

"This is the best thing we've ever done."

"I'm no good, Ben."

"Cynthia, enough."

"I only thought I loved you. And then he wrote me that check. The only thing that rivaled us was the memory of holding that check in my hand. All those zeroes. It was so plain. I get checks like that all the time now, and I still remember it."

"I understand."

"How can you?"

"You don't think I've seen what money does to people? To grown men, twice your age? The spell that comes over them? You were young. And you had nothing."

"I didn't give you a second look. I walked right out of that building and I didn't even give you a first look, let alone a second."

"You took the money and invested it. You became independent. Made something of yourself, and then fucking paid it back. You, Miss Gordon, are not 'no good.'"

Cynthia felt the bile of unspoken things rising up her esophagus. If she sits on them any longer, they could officially be considered lies. She swallows, tamping them down for the moment.

"I'm starting to hate your father," she says.

"Don't. It's not a good path. Trust me."

"He took away ten years of our life."

"He gave you ten years of yours."

"It was a curse. I sold my soul. Like that Faustian deal you talked about once."

"He knew what a deal like that would do to a person like you. The money was just the sleight of hand."

She shook her head woefully as he continued to defend her.

"He told me if I tried to contact you he could sue me. Ruin my career, follow me, make me unemployable. Or I could just... take the money and run. And I believed him. He was so full of shit. I'm sure it worked better than even he thought it would."

"He wasn't full of shit."

"What?"

"He would've done everything he said. It would've been like... smashing an ant with your thumb."

Cynthia just lays there as he strokes her arm.

"I just realized something," he chuckles.

"What?"

"You haven't given me an answer," he grins.

Cynthia was quiet, so much so that he thought she was asleep.

"Cynthia?"

She raised up to look at him, giving his face a once over as though her time with him was limited.

"Cynthia, please don't tell me I've just made a fool of myself."

Something prevented him from pressing the issue. She laid her head back down on his chest, stroking the fine hairs there.

"Let's not ruin this. Later, I promise."

* * *

"He's in and out today," Ben's sister Val says.

It's the beginning of the end when Ben comes over to his father's penthouse to meet with Val, and thanks to his reunion with Cynthia the night before, it doesn't completely railroad him.

As much as he's come to resent him, seeing his father lose the savvy that he's come to rely on is not something he takes joy in. He wants to, but the sight is too sobering, watching such a man become a humiliation, an imbecile. Ben wants no part of that karmic fate.

"I think I'd like to see him," Ben suddenly says. Val looks at him with surprise.

Ever since Cynthia re-entered his life he's felt a need to talk to the old man as much as possible, to unlock this piece of the past as foggy as his own father's head. All the answers are in there. And they are ironically locked away in a mental safe so secure that even his father can't get back into it.

"You wanna know something Dad? Before last night, I would've come in here, saying the worst possible things I could think of, hoping you could understand them and not be able to do anything about it. No snappy remarks. No smug response about how this family owes you our unquestioned devotion. You'd be left alone while my awful words swirled around in your brain and came out at the strangest, most disjointed of times.

"But last night, I was with Cynthia. And it made me realize something. You're just one man. And you can't stop me, or anyone else. With all your resources. Sure you can delay things. Can cause unforeseen obstacles. But it only causes things to come back stronger. You can't stop anything or anyone. You're no match for life."

Ben pulls his chair close up to his father as he sits in his rocker facing the window.

"Making me wait ten years was the best thing you could've done for me. You know that? Now I know what I want. It's the same thing I always wanted, but now I know for sure. I said I was going to find Cynthia, and it took me a long time, but I did it. And now I have your company. And there isn't a thing you can do to me. I got everything I set out to get. And it's even better than I thought. So in a roundabout way, I'm grateful. Thank you, Dad."

"Cynthia?" his father suddenly says.

Ben goes cold and stiff. Was his father having a lucid moment?

"Cynthia Gordon. The designer. The girl I was in love with. You paid her $100,000 to stay away from me. Well, she finally paid you back. She paid you back and then some."

"Her mother..." he begins, tearing up like an old woman.

Ben shivers from head to toe.

"Her mother? What about her mother?"

"She mustn't find out. Did she receive the flowers?"

"Did who? Cynthia's mother?"

"No, she's *dead*, don't you know that! No, the *girl*! Such a beautiful girl. Just beautiful," his father confesses with a far off look. The uncharacteristic moment catches Ben off guard.

"She's even more beautiful now," Ben replies. "Think you can make it to the wedding?" he dares with dark humor.

All of a sudden his eyes meet his son's steadily. Ben shudders uncontrollably.

"You weren't supposed to find out. I went too far. I went too far..."

Ben desperately wants Val, anyone, to come barging into the room. He's suddenly afraid of his own father but he doesn't move.

191

"Went too far with what, Dad?"

"I can't tell you. You'll tell her. And she mustn't find out."

"Cynthia?"

His father nods quickly.

"Everything I built... it will go to the girl anyway. Isn't that true?"

Ben sighs, hearing his father refer to Cynthia as his shrunken mind remembers her.

"It will. All that scheming was in vain, Dad."

"You would've left me. It was the best way. You weren't supposed to find out."

Ben clenches and unclenches his fists, his jaw, before he continues.

"All that scheming," Ben repeats, shaking his head, a tremble in his lip. His father's state was almost too humbling. "You should've lived a good life, Dad. The very moment you pissed in your own hallway. That should've been the time to start re-evaluating. But no. You were too arrogant. Even for that. And now look at us. We can't even carry on a conversation. I'll never know what it is you have to tell me."

14

Ten Years Ago

Solomon Dvorak was a shrewd man. A wealthy man. And he got that way by manipulating everything and everyone around him. He knew best. Knows best. And right now, his 2nd oldest's future was in jeopardy.

He let himself be suckered in by his compassion. Watching Benjamin bravely undergo surgery after surgery. Letting the physical therapists work his atrophying limbs this way and that while he screamed in agony, determined to prove the medical experts wrong.

He'd withheld his discipline, and now he was paying for it.

Solomon could still manipulate Benjamin's motivations, however. He was surprised to learn that the root of them was fear. Of being abandoned, of being rejected. He came by it honestly, he was his mother's child, after all. Once Solomon could convince Ben that he was disposable, he was an asset in a way that Grant could never be.

Grant knew from the beginning his worth to the Dvorak legacy, a rookie mistake on Solomon's record. He did not make the same mistake with Ben. Why become attached to a child constantly teetering on the verge of death?

Ben practically killed himself proving his worth to his father, the company, to everyone. Word was getting back to him how well Ben was doing downstairs. He worked every bit as hard and as long as anyone else. Never complained, got along well with the other associates, and never leaned on the Dvorak name to get things done.

And all that was fine, fine. Good for him.

But he apparently had taken a liking to a certain cafeteria worker.

Were it a one-time thing, he could've overlooked the fireable offense. But it seems now they were fraternizing, and his sources were telling him that it was escalating. Quickly.

Eventually, Benjamin of course would have to marry. But not for love. Not for any of the things that young men marry for.

He was a junior analyst, and if he was to become a senior associate, then senior VP, and finally president, then there would be no time for honeymoons or vacations, or even coming home for dinner. He didn't understand how Ben, as smart as he was, could look at this vast empire and think he could run it by punching a clock and being average.

This woman, whoever she was, was average. She worked 40 hours a week and came back day after day because it was the best she could do. And he didn't need this average woman, filling his son's head with average ideas. Like settling down, and working less, and "money isn't everything."

Money isn't everything. For fuck's sake. Of course, money isn't *everything*. And when you have a shitload of it, quaint platitudes such as those are suicide.

"Sir, I have Cynthia Gordon waiting for you," his secretary warbled through the phone.

"Very well, send her in," Solomon bellowed.

Solomon knew he would never be able to convince his son to do what's best for himself. Once he got something in his mind, any protest was like cement for his feet.

But perhaps he could convince the young lady to do what's best. Average though she may be, it didn't mean that she was an idiot.

His office door creaked open and in walked the beautiful young girl from the associate's party that had caught his son's eye months before— and Solomon's radar. Jewish she most certainly was not. This little low-class goyim habit Benjamin had was the act of a lifetime of spite, Solomon was certain.

"Cynthia. Please have a seat."

"I'd rather stand, sir."

Solomon cracked a smile.

Ben must be divulging all kinds of things to the girl for her to have so little sense of respect for where she was.

"Very well, Miss Gordon. Any idea why you're here?"

"I imagine it has something to do with Benji."

"Benji?"

"Benjamin. Your son?"

"My son." Solomon Dvorak paused as he sat back in his chair. "What else has Mr. Dvorak told you? About his place in the company?"

"He doesn't talk to me about work."

Oh, for heaven's sake.

"With all due respect, Miss Gordon, this 'work' is his life."

"Is that why you have us followed?"

So she wasn't an idiot. Good.

"I like to keep tabs on all my employees. Including my son. Including you, Miss Gordon."

195

Cynthia was poker-faced.

"My cafeteria manager tells me that you've been having someone else punch your timecard in the mornings."

"Jorge? But why would he—"

"And someone else to punch your card in the evenings. I'm sure you know from your employee handbook that this is a serious violation of our code of conduct."

"That's a lie. You're lying," she blurted. Solomon's entourage bristled, but he did not.

"Be careful who you accuse, Miss Gordon."

"Look, I'm telling your son it's over if that's what this is about."

Solomon was surprised, but he continued unphased.

"We don't engage in unethical practices at the Dvorak group. This is merely a meeting about your performance. And your inevitable termination."

Cynthia let a bit of panic seep into her words, an effort to appeal to his compassion, perhaps.

"Mr. Dvorak, please. Sir, I need this job."

"I sympathize," he said, though his body language suggested otherwise, "but the two of you working at the same company has clearly compromised your judgment. And his. Falsifying your timesheet is a fireable offense."

"But I didn't! Sir, there must be some way that I can prove—"

"All discharged employees are required to sign a non-disclosure agreement when they leave the Dvorak Group. You'll be provided with a sizeable severance package, which is not normally offered to our hourly employees, so consider yourself very special. I've been told you'll be very difficult to replace."

Cynthia's steely blue-gray eyes turned fiery.

"What if I say no?"

The deafening silence in the room had his junior VP associates eyeing each other.

"Say no to what, Miss Gordon?"

"What if I don't sign? What if I tell Benji about this little meeting?"

The deafening silence suddenly turned a bit amused. His junior VP gave a smirk.

"Well, first things first, Miss Gordon," he said, sitting up in his chair. "Let's see, if you don't sign, then your termination becomes a resignation. And an employee who quits will get nothing. Also, I don't take kindly to threats, and seeing as how you need this job, as you said, I'm sure you'll need every other job just as much. I can very easily make an uncooperative, insubordinate employee like yourself *un*employable, Miss Gordon."

"I see. And what about the part where Ben finds out about all this?"

Solomon Dvorak gave her a smile. Only vaguely resembling his son's.

"I understand that you and your mother live in a van just outside of Jersey City," Solomon said.

Cynthia's heartbeat doubled. She tried to hide the wild fear coursing through her, succeeding except for her eyes.

"You haven't told him, have you? That you're homeless. Why is that?"

Cynthia didn't answer.

"I don't say any of this to scare you, Miss Gordon. Just so that you can properly understand the scope of what you're dealing with here. Clearly being on the top floor of the Dvorak Group building, in the office of its owner doesn't mean much."

"No, it doesn't. Because you're a cunt. And I can call you that to your face, because I have nothing, and I don't care.

Meanwhile, you're a slave, which is why you have to pay me money."

Solomon laughed, perhaps more than anyone had ever seen him laugh. The rest of the room was in hushed awe.

Not only was he assured he was doing the right thing, Solomon realized he'd narrowly dodged a bullet.

They were sleeping together. More than that. This young girl would be the death of his son, the death of everything he worked for.

"I can see why my son is so smitten with you, Miss Gordon. He has a habit of... collecting the people he likes. Using his wealth and resources to keep them close. He has nothing else, you see. Not in his mind. In his mind, he'll always be a cripple."

"That's not true."

"Did my son tell you he was engaged?"

Her sudden silence answered his question.

Oh, Benjamin. His flimsy backbone was about to do Solomon's hard work for him.

"My son is a good man. Committed to the task of being honorable. But he is spoiled. An oversight on my part, I'm afraid. He has never been poor. He hasn't the faintest idea of it. I'm sure you know precisely what I mean."

"What do you know about it? You inherited this company just as he will," Cynthia retorted.

"I did. But before my dad nearly drove himself mad to become the sort of man that you have to become, to make a fortune in this world out of nothing, we knew a level of poverty that doesn't exist in many places anymore."

Suddenly, he reached into the center drawer of his desk and pulled out what looked to be a checkbook.

"Not only am I going to offer you a severance package, Miss

Gordon, I'm going to write you a check."

"Mr. Dvorak—"

"Call me Sol. Please. Take me up on the deal. I don't offer it to many."

She watched him scribble from his chair, unable to make out the amount, but it looked very large.

"Is it true you were going to tell my son that it was over?"

"Yes."

"Why?"

"Because it... it would never work," she admitted cryptically. She didn't want to give him the satisfaction of knowing the real reason, the one they were currently discussing.

Solomon Dvorak smiled. "Believe it or not, Cynthia, I'm beginning to like you. You're smart. And because of this, you deserve to learn a particular lesson, as early as possible." He slid the check at the edge of the desk, urging her to take it.

"You'll cancel it as soon as I walk out the door."

"I'll do no such thing."

"Why?"

"Because my son has toyed with you terribly, I'm afraid. You're not the first casualty of his. A little known habit he's acquired. And I'd like to keep it that way."

"...Or else you'll ruin me," Cynthia wilted, piecing together the true nature of the Dvoraks.

"Among other things. Money has a way of appeasing a woman scorned, I've found. Despite the nature of this meeting, I hope you understand that I wish you well."

Cynthia picked up the check laying on his desk.

"Oddly, I do."

"You've officially become an investment of mine. And I like to keep track of all my investments, as you can imagine, Miss

Gordon."

She studied the check as though it were an alien artifact. She looked at her name next to the large sum. *A hundred thousand isn't a lot these days*, she tried to tell herself.

"I'll pay this back. If it takes me my whole life I will."

"I look forward to it. But if you so much as send him an e-mail, I'll find out. And that will be your undoing."

"You won't get away with this."

"We'll see. Oh, and don't spend it all in one place, Miss Gordon. I'll not have it in the budget for more."

* * *

Cynthia waited three hours on the steps of the shelter where her mother was staying, and where she was on schedule to pick up the keys to their apartment in the next two weeks.

The three hours went by fast. Cynthia was in a stupor, mentally reliving her and Ben's relationship, now seeing the obvious truth. She replayed Melanie's visit, where Cynthia remembered a flash of the gleaming ring on Melanie's hand. One that must've been so old that she didn't feel the need to flaunt it.

He was playing me. Oh God, was he playing me, she kept saying over and over to herself. A wave of nausea washed over her and she fought off tears when she saw the van pulling around the entrance. Bev gave her a smile that rapidly turned to a look of motherly concern.

"Whatcha doing here, gyal?"

"I got fired."

"Jus' so?? Why?"

"They said I had someone punching my time card."

"Fuh true? Did you?"

"No, Mama."

"Yuh can' lettem *bad talk you*, Cynt'ya!"

"They gave me a severance. A big one."

"Severance?"

Cynthia showed her mother the check.

"Whutta Benji say? His faddah run the place, ent?"

"His 'faddah' wrote deh check, Mama."

Bev took the check from her hand and examined it.

"Deh man put dis in yuh hand, Cynt'ya?"

"Yes."

"Why? He writin' personal checks to a *gyal*, eh? Does Benji know 'dat?"

"Benji wasn't there," Cynthia cryptically replied.

"Yuh not stayin' wit' im no more?"

"No, Mama. We broke up."

"Yuh don' make sense, gyal—"

"Benji is engaged! To be married. He didn't tell me! I had to find out from his father! Everyone warned me about him, but I didn't listen. I don't wanna talk about it anymore, I don't wanna be there anymore, he offered me severance and I took it. Okay? Now 'den, do yuh wanna hear deh plan, awat?"

"Who ask you 'dat," Bev slowly said with her eyes narrowed on her daughter, her hands slowly going to her hips. "Now I'm sorry to hear about yuh Benji. I liked dat boy. But get 'dat *back chat* outcha voice an '*den* tell me de plan, gyal."

Bev was able to get back the rent money she saved but her deposit to the apartment was lost. But for the first time in a long time, it was a hill of beans rather than a crippling setback.

They found themselves back in the van, but only temporarily. Cynthia was a wreck. She had a constant onset of jitters that couldn't subside, not to mention a wicked broken heart, and a horrid personal rain cloud of guilt each time she tried to cheer herself up with the money or her tidy severance package.

She couldn't sleep and when she did, she woke up in cold sweats, expecting to wake up in a modest high rise looking up at a vaulted ceiling, only to again be greeted by the sight of the felt fabric of the van's ceiling, which only caused her more disorientation. Were those six months at the Dvorak group, those months in Ben's arms, even real? Without the check, she would've had no proof.

Most days, she hoped it truly all was a dream, just so she didn't have to face this unknown future suddenly alone and cold. The thought of food repulsed her, she started to lose weight. Her life had become an excruciating series of baby steps. If she could just make it all the way to Jersey where her mother was. Then if they could just make it to the bank. Then if they could just get the check to clear.

Bev suggested Cynthia sit down with a manager and let him handle the check, rather than going through the line. Even then they were told to "wait right here" at least a half dozen times while phone calls were made and numbers were triple checked. It could've been racist, but Cynthia got the feeling that having an amount of money like that released to anyone was bound to be an ordeal. Finally, Cynthia suggested they call him directly.

"I think Sol would prefer this to be handled as discreetly as possible," Cynthia suggested. She couldn't know what they were thinking she meant by that, but finally someone drummed up the courage to take her advice, and they were out of there in the next twenty minutes.

She opened an account while she was there just to make things easy. If the account went under $10,000, she would be charged a significant penalty. The plan was to buy a house at auction for no more than $30,000 and put no more than $50,000 into it. They simply could not go over budget. Cynthia would find another job, put off school a little longer and... the plan stopped there. They were free to live in the moment rather than swing from vine to circumstantial vine. If they could just get the right house.

"The next property up for auction is 324 Indigo Drive, 3 bedroom 2 bath, 1421 square feet, bidding starts at $15,000."

A week later they were at the Jersey Home Auction house.

"$15,000," Cynthia piped up in front of the auctioneer.

"You can just raise your hand, sweethawt," the auctioneer informed her.

A few others raised their hands until only two bidders were left, Cynthia and another gentleman who looked like he knew his way around an auction. The auction went on tediously in thousand dollar increments. The housing market was still no where near recovery, only the risktakers and people with piles of cash were left.

"$40,000," Cynthia suddenly said. Her mother grabbed her arm. With that, her opponent instantly backed off.

"Sold!" said the auctioneer.

"Looks like our budget just shrunk a bit," Bev muttered.

"But we got it, Mama! It's ours. And no one can take it from us," Cynthia smiled. She took her hand and gave it a victory squeeze.

Her opponent came up to them and shook their hands, a young looking guy who looked more like a former gang member than someone who would be at a house auction.

"You lovely ladies overpaid, you know that, right?"

"It was worth it," Cynthia smiled.

"You must be an owner-occupant."

"I am."

"Well, I like to do a little research before these things. I've lived in Jersey my whole life, I know the city, and I know this house. It's gonna need some work."

"We know, we're prepeared."

"Well, if you ever need help, I know a lot of good reputable contractors and such. And in a few years, you'll probably want to sell."

"Trust us. We ain't *nevah* movin' again, Dan," Bev laughed.

"Still. You never know," the man said, retrieving a card from his pocket.

"Gabriel Alvarez," Cynthia read the name.

"That's me."

"Nice to meet you, Gabriel," she said as they shook hands.

"Everyone calls me Gabe."

They got back in the van, just a van again and not a house, for the first time in two years. They pulled up to the modest little yellow property in Hoboken with the bay window, modest yard, and a towering tree that was sure to be a beautiful source of shade in summer.

The house had no keys, so they essentially they had to break in. Luckily the back door was open.

The house had been winterized and was as cold on the inside as it was outside. When they walked in, they couldn't believe their eyes. Glass all over the floor. The hardwood had been deliberately damaged. Paint all over the countertops.

"Whappen here? Likkle *jhanjats* knockin' about, lookin' fuh melee, awat?"

"Not likely. Look."

Bev turned to look at the living room wall where "F u c k P e n n y - W i l d e" was spray-painted in big black garish letters, the name of the lender that repossessed Bev's house and apparently this one too.

"Anudda satisfied customer, 'den."

"Shit."

"We needed 'dat extra $10,000, Cynt'ya."

"We woulda lost the house, Mama."

"Yuh heard de man. He said we overpaid!"

"For an investor, Mama! He's just gonna get another house at another auction. But this is our home. We don't have deadlines, we got time, and we still got plenty of budget. We replace the windows, paint the walls, fill in every scratch in this floor if we have to. We fight up, we'll be fine."

The tour of the house got a little more dismal the more they looked. Tons of trash and clothing were left behind. The previous owner even took their rage out on the plumbing system and poured concrete down the toilets and sinks. When they opened the refrigerator it was still full of food from God only knows when. At least it was January and not July. Cynthia instantly bolted out the back door at the sight, vomiting and retching in the backyard. Bev slowly followed her out and knelt beside her with trepidation.

"Yuh need t'go to the hospital Cynt'ya."

"I'm fine. It's that fucking refrigerator, it's disgusting."

"Yuh haven't *eaten* since you and Benji broke up," Bev replied.

"I've just been anxious since I got this money that something will go wrong, that's all. And now we have a house. It's a mess, but that's okay. We're here. It's over. Besides, we don't even have insurance."

Bev sighed. That's when she had to admit that she'd failed as a parent. Cynthia's burden was much too high and heavy.

Not to mention she was starting to suspect her sudden onset of sickness was more than just a broken heart and "anxiety." Lord, she hoped Winston wasn't watching right now, God rest his soul.

"Whut yuh got looks like more 'dan just *tabanka* Cynti. Leh we go. Now fuh now."

Cynthia was in no state to argue. Whatever she'd thrown up couldn't have been food. She was jittery and probably dehydrated. Wobbly, she got on her feet, leaning on her mother as they got back in the van. Even though the house had been a sitting mess that she'd never laid eyes on before today, she drove away worried that they were leaving the doors unlocked. She smiled. Next order of business was to call a locksmith.

15

Present Day

"**M**s. Gordon, Mr. Dvorak is here to see you."

"Now? In the lobby?"

"Yes ma'am. Shall I send him your way?"

"No, I'm coming out. Thanks, Jeanine."

Cynthia feels a flurry of butterflies, a now common occurrence as she wordlessly gets up from her desk and half jogs her way to the lobby, where Ben is standing before her, smiling and holding a bouquet of flowers. The butterflies in her stomach become bees. Killer bees.

"Ben? What are you doing here?"

"You don't sound happy to see me."

"No... just surprised."

He gives her a kiss on the cheek. Slowly she closes her eyes.

"I can come back."

"No, it's... a good a time as any, I guess. Hold my calls, Jeanine. And put these in water."

The walk down the hallway seems as unusually long as it is quiet.

"Don't think I haven't noticed the strategic location of your office, Miss Gordon."

She looks over her shoulder with a fond grin, stopping just before the door to give him another kiss.

"I thought you might," she smiled. "I made sure it was well insulated."

"Care to test it out?"

"Another time."

When they walk through the double doors to her spacious office, Ben is startled to see a little white girl with long legs, taking up considerable room on the roomy tufted couch in the corner.

Her hair is long and straight, almost stringy. She is watching some mysterious show on a medium sized tablet that seems to be about fashion.

For a good ten seconds, he is utterly clueless. Ten measly seconds, between the past and reality, before the world comes crashing down on him weighty and overwhelming. Like suddenly falling between one of the cracks in the Grand Canyon.

When Cynthia sees the knowing come across his face, she is utterly devastated. She has no words, so she sits behind her desk and holds back her emotion as much as she can for the sake of her daughter, who has absolutely no clue what is going on.

Ben still hasn't moved. He is staring and staring. He spent enough time in the mirror to know what his own eyes look like, and she had them. He asks the question anyway.

"Who's this?"

"This is Ella," Cynthia announced shakily.

Eventually, Ella realizes this is no ordinary meeting at her mom's office, and that Ben certainly looks like no ordinary client.

She sits up, looking alarmed as if she has failed to prepare for something. She looks to her mother for guidance, who isn't much help, her own face raw with emotion. She looks up at the gentleman who is looking at her, the two of them looking at her in the same way and she comes to the logical conclusion. They are a family.

"Is this...is he my..." she finds herself afraid to say the word in case he was a stranger. She wells up at the very dilemma, relieved when her mother instantly begins nodding emphatically.

She told Ella they would meet soon. She hadn't wanted to traumatize either of them. But she's realizing now that that was impossible.

Ben gets down painfully on one knee, almost instinctively, so that he is just below her eye level. Ella openly weeps as she wraps her arms around Ben's neck without any emotional barriers.

Cynthia is being stabbed with knives. She watches as her daughter's apparently secret and desperate dream comes true, a dream that Cynthia has denied her. She can't decipher Ben's face, which is obscured by Ella's arms draped over his shoulders. He slowly caresses her back with his big hands in a downward motion, instantly communicating that he is here now, and that is how it was going to be. Slowly her sobs of relief subside.

Cynthia too is lulled into a sense of security. Maybe this is going to be okay. Maybe he wouldn't be angry with her. Maybe...

But the guilty rot in her stomach overwhelms her, and she is suddenly locked out of their sweet reunion.

"Ell, let me and your father talk for a second," she says while Ella wipes her face.

"Unfortunately, I have to leave," he says, without looking at Cynthia. Ella's silent distress washes over him like a tidal wave.

"But I'll be back, okay?" he directs at Ella. He touches her face as he looks in her eyes, until the fear in her expression is replaced with trust. Ella nods.

"Can I come see you tomorrow?" he asks. She nods again, giving a little laugh.

Cynthia gets up from her chair and goes around her desk as Ben is slowly back up on his feet.

"I'll walk you out," she says.

He doesn't answer as he heads for the door, Cynthia hurrying on his heels.

Slowly she closes the office door behind her and rushes down the hallway to keep up with him. He sure was fast, for a guy with a limp.

"I was going to tell you," Cynthia tries to assuage him in a low voice. "After the reveal. I had to prepare her, Ben."

Ben stops. He turns to look at her, his eyes filled with condemnation, as though her very words astound him at their selfishness. She doesn't know if he's expecting her to keep talking, or if he's going to hit her.

"He told me what would happen if I contacted you," she barely eeks.

Ben turns around and commences walking, down the hallway, across the lobby and out the door. Cynthia follows behind him, waiting until they are outside, out of earshot of her receptionist before she continues.

"You said it yourself, he could smush us like an ant."

"That's his *grand*daughter, Cynthia. He's not a monster."

Cynthia stops walking, but Ben doesn't.

"He knew," Cynthia says to his back.

Ben stops and slowly turns around.

"What?" he furrows his brow, walking back towards her.

"He found out. Of course, he found out!"

"I don't believe you," he says, breathing as though he would pass out. They were practically nose to nose.

"You think I built all this in five years with just 100 grand??" she snipes in a low tone as if terrified anyone else but the two of them could hear. When it's clear she has his attention, she continues.

"That day in his office... I signed a non-disclosure. But there wasn't anything in it about a baby. I didn't find out myself until a few weeks later. I tried to keep it secret as long as I could. I wore baggy clothes, I barely went out because I figured out he was still having me followed.

"When Ella was born he... I got home from the hospital and there were flowers. He sent us money. *Lots* of money," she whispered, choked up as if right back there again. "If I didn't spend it, he sent more. If I didn't cash the checks, he wired it. He was fucked and he knew it. It was getting out of his control. It freaked us out how much he was freaked out."

"So you kept taking the money, and you kept my daughter from me."

Cynthia takes a breath, waiting to see if Ben will let her explain. She doesn't want to. Her mouth fills with excuses and she wants to throw up.

"Mom started getting sick..." it pains Cynthia to acknowledge, to relive, but she needs him to understand. "She couldn't work, she didn't have insurance... she didn't even want to go to the hospital, she just wanted to spend as much time with Ella as she could before she..." her voice trails off, and for a moment Ben thinks she might actually throw up.

"He paid for the treatments. He paid for everything. So she could be home. And then when she... I wasn't planning on being some big-time designer. I sold the house for triple what we bought it for, and I figured I could do the same thing again and again. I didn't have a choice, really. I was 22 and the only person I had *in the world* was gone. School was definitely off the table after all that. I couldn't *stand* getting handouts from your father. I vowed to pay him back and he just kept making the debt unpayable. It was unbearable. Whatever I didn't use to start Indigo Properties went into a trust fund for Ella."

"I don't hear anything about you contacting me."

"...I couldn't risk it until I knew we were safe. Until Indigo Properties was safe."

"Ten *years*, Cynthia? Ten."

"You kept getting engaged, the Dvorak Group was always in the news. Sometimes I would see you on the street—"

"That's your excuse? You thought I was, what, too unstable?"

"If you would've rejected her, then I would've literally had to kill you," Cynthia patiently tries to explain, her hands pressed together as if in prayer. "I would've risked putting my neck out there for nothing, and then I would've had to kill you, if your dad didn't kill me first. And then I would be in jail and she would have no one. It was just easier for you to not know."

"Ten *years!* Cynthia!" he exclaims, his tone is so mournful that Cynthia's heart breaks.

"He made me think you were the bad guy, that you toyed with women like me all the time..."

"That's what he said?"

"He said I wasn't the first he had to pay hush money to."

"Holy fucking shit, I can't believe this..." Ben puts a hand to his head, dizzy with rage.

"He only implied it. I filled in the rest. For years, I didn't even question it. I'm sorry, Ben. I was all alone, I had to think of myself. We needed the money."

"The money."

"Yes, the *money*, Ben!" Cynthia explodes. "I can't raise a kid on *hopes*! The extortion money went straight into the house, it was a vandalized mess! Mom couldn't work once it was done, then she got sick, and I was *pregnant*!! I didn't know what kind of man you were, you could've disowned her! I couldn't take the risk!"

"That's *bull*shit, Cynthia. *Fuck* him. You *knew* me. Better than he did."

"I didn't," she replied as he began to walk away again. She followed behind, close on his heels.

"You've always known me."

"I wasn't so sure."

"You're *worse* than him."

"That's not fair," Cynthia cried.

"All he had was money. You think it does him a bit of good now?"

"I was angry too, Ben. You were engaged the *whole time* we were... you made me think that was real—"

"It *was* real!!" he roared.

Cynthia was quiet.

"I didn't know that."

"He couldn't take away memories, Cynthia. Only *you* could do that. You denied me a life I'll never have. You denied me everything. You knew better, and you *robbed* me."

"I *know* that. I saw that little girl's face in there, and I know that now, and I am... *sorry*. Okay?"

"How can you say that you love me?"

"Oh, God, poor *you*!" Cynthia sniped. "Honestly, if you hadn't shown up out of the blue, you wouldn't have found out until she showed up at your door on her 18th birthday. Because *that's* when I was going to tell her!"

Her words sting. Instantly she wants to retract them. A lump forms in her throat. She was kidding herself to think this could end any other way.

"Sorry, I didn't mean... I had to choose between you and her, okay? I couldn't have both."

"I'll be back tomorrow. Same time. Just make sure she's here," Ben answers stoically.

Cynthia swallows. So that's it then. She can hear the crackling sound of his proposal drying up and blowing away with loathing. She asked him to promise not to hate her, but she had no right to do that. Not without him knowing. Her heart feels as though it's been burned.

"You could pick her up from school if you want. 2:30. You can bring her here," she volunteers.

"Even better."

"I couldn't take the risk, Benji."

"I get it, okay? I still don't want to hear anymore. I can't," he scoffs as he got in his BMW.

"PS 9," she says.

The same school he'd gone to at her age. Has he told her that? He stops, just as he was about to start the car.

"Really?"

Cynthia quickly nods, emotion welling up.

She must've remembered. He'd been blocks away from her for five years. The notion only makes him sick as he wordlessly puts the car in gear and drives away.

* * *

"Ella."

That was the name his father was mysteriously crying out he

214

realizes on the way to his father's apartment, the name of his granddaughter. "*Everything I built will all go to the girl anyway*," he'd said.

He wasn't speaking of Cynthia, he was speaking of Ella. He *had* known. "*I went too far… I went too far…*"

And the lie kept snowballing, bigger and faster, while he lived his life oblivious. *"Promise you won't hate me…"*

The traffic is horrendous on the way to his father's apartment, so Ben can barely keep his emotions together on his way there. Like nature calling without a place to go in sight, Ben completely loses it only a block away from his destination. Gripping the steering wheel, he unleashes obscenity-laden screams into the plush interior of his car. He pounds the dashboard again and again thinking of his formless, odorless lifelong prison that kept running long after its warden was incapacitated, so thorough was his control.

Finally Ben gets to the penthouse apartment and barges in unannounced.

"Ben? Oh my God, what's wrong?" Valerie asks, startled.

"It's worse than I thought, Val. It's so much worse."

Val rises from her sitting position on the couch. Rosa looks on with a furrowed brow of concern as he pushes past her at the door, barreling towards the upstairs.

"Where is he?"

"In his room."

Without warning or hesitation, Ben opens his father's bedroom door.

"Dad."

His dad looks up at him from his bed, a violent lack of recognition in his eyes. Ben ignores the scene, the question of his being confined to the bed, the sound of monitors.

"I saw Ella today, Dad."

No response.

"You know, the girl whose name you scream in the night? Because you're a tortured *fuck*?"

"Ben!" Val barges in. She grabs Ben by the arm but he's stiff as a tree and radiating anger.

"You won, Dad. You did. I didn't want to admit it, but... before I even set my mind to beat you, you'd already gone lower than I ever gave you credit for. And you know what? I give. I'm out. I can't play this game. I can't even think about everything you stole from me, or else I won't be able to function. But the good part is, I can't do another thing, that I don't want to do, for someone else. I don't want to do this job, I don't want to be your son, and I don't want a single cent of your ill-gotten money."

With that, Ben gives his father a final look before he simply turns and walks out.

Val exchanges a vacant look with her father before she turns to follow him. She doesn't have to go far to find him slumped over the upstairs balcony railing, staring straight ahead out of the loft windows.

"Ben? What's going on?"

"What's going on is I have a daughter, Val. She's nine years old. Her name's Ella. I just met her today. Because Dad intimidated Cynthia, to the point where she felt completely alone and couldn't come to me. And honestly, I'm starting to think he killed her mother or something."

"Okay... slow down. Cynthia has a daughter?"

"She was pregnant. When she left. He didn't know that. Neither did she. Otherwise, he probably would've suicided her."

"Relax, Ben. Dad's no monster, and you're not that important."

"That's what I said! You know the extortion was just the beginning? You know he had her followed, for *years*? When her mother got sick, he knew about it. He paid for her treatments. Why would he do that, Val?"

"You just found this out today?"

"Today."

"You met this girl?"

"Yes."

"And you're sure she's yours?"

At that Ben nods his head, a grimace on his face as he breaks down, covering his face with his hand.

Val feels a painful lump in her throat watching her brother cry with what has to be a mixture of elation and heartache.

Ben would've been overjoyed as a young father. Definitely one of those that obsessed over every milestone. Probably would prefer to have a son, but who knows. A little girl... my word!

Certainly, he wouldn't have risen up the ranks so fast at the Dvorak Group. Probably wouldn't have spent all his waking and sleeping hours there.

She knows what he's saying is true, and she's torn between the love she is re-discovering for her father and the pain of his past actions that he's spread and inflicted. Dad overplayed his hand. Now he's lost Ben forever.

She's never seen her brother in such anguish and she embraces him, knowing that closure for him will likely be impossible.

"Grant's supposed to be in town this weekend," she says.

"Grant? For what?" he sniffs.

"...I'm moving him to hospice."

Ben responds with a stoic quiet, sensitive to his sister's grief that he now notices is radiating from her pores.

"When were you going to tell me?"

"Today," she mutters. "Ella. That's the girl's name?"

He nods, still in each other's arms.

"You think they ever met?"

"I don't know."

"Find out. If she has anything to say to him, now's the time. Cynthia too for that matter."

16

Present Day

Ben takes the subway two stops and walks until he is standing outside of his old school amongst a gaggle of other parents, waiting for Ella to be let out. He doesn't worry much about being bothered or recognized for who he is, especially in the city, but his shabby chic wardrobe choice of dress slacks and a plain graphic t-shirt probably hurt more than it helped. The moms seem to be craning their necks to get a good look at him.

"You're new," one of the women piped up.

"I am," he smiled.

"Divorced?"

"...More like... estranged," he answers, not quite sure why he feels the need to explain himself to this strange lady who is probably judging him, or being nosy about his relationship status. And yet part of him wants to be asked about it, so that he can talk about his daughter.

"Oh!" she exclaims, apparently not expecting a genuine answer. "Well. Good for you for making an effort. Hopefully you won't be a stranger," she says, in a mom-flirt tone.

"I definitely won't," he responds, hoping she didn't get the wrong idea by his answer.

His heart is thumping in his chest and his emotions have been all over the place since yesterday. Every time he tried to feel the sheer joy of being a father, the tail end of loss built up over ten years practically constricted his arteries with bitterness and trauma. At any point, could he have opened his eyes and figured it out for himself?

He hears the dull roar of students after the ring of a final bell that reminds him a bit of a cattle call. Children of different ages pool out of the front doors and he can't control his ache. The pre-schoolers, the kindergartners, the ages he missed and will never get back. They jump in the arms of their parents with oversized, colorful backpacks as big as them, their short stubby hands engulfed in those of their mothers.

His heartbeat intensifies, worrying about etiquette. Should he hug her or... wave? Should he even be awkwardly searching for her in the crowd?

Finally, he spots her, thankful to just get it over with and face his anxiety. She's looking around, and they finally lock eyes. His smile is instant, uncontrollable. Ella beams, shyly making her way towards him.

"Hi, Dad!"

"Hi."

"Ella Gordon is your daughter??" the strange woman asks, surprised.

"Yep, Ms. Meville. This is my dad."

"Well, well. Doesn't that explain quite a bit!" Ms. Melville's surprise melts into warm excitement. "Tell your mom I said, 'you win again.' She'll know what I mean."

"Okay," Ella chuckled, she and Ben having only a vague

understanding.

Ella smiles big again and grabs Ben for a hug. Instead of strange, it instantly feels natural and secure. Real. She grabs onto his arm and eventually his hand, tight, as if they hadn't just met yesterday.

Her affection is brazen and forceful enough to send a lesser man running, even though she has the prudence of her mother, he can tell. He smiles, melting. In five minutes he confronts the first rule of parenting, which is regular rules don't apply to your kids.

"Your mom tell you I was picking you up?"

"Yeah."

"....Wanna go somewhere?"

"I thought you're taking me to mom's office?"

"I am. Eventually."

She smiled.

"Um... my mom sometimes takes me to get ice cream."

"Near the Chinese restaurant?"

"How'd you know?"

"I used to meet your mom there all the time."

"She told me."

"She did?" he smiles. She nods, returning it.

* * *

"So what else did your mom tell you about me?"

Ben and Ella are a block away from the Dvorak building, where he is currently playing hookey while he puts his brain pieces back together. He doesn't know what's happening there right now, and he doesn't care. They sit across from each other at a small round table, each of them nursing sundaes with long spoons in front of the circular window facing the New Yorkers trekking the wide, continuous sidewalks.

"Just that you guys used to work together at the same place. That's how you met."

"That's it?"

"Well, basically. But I started asking her more and more questions. Once I got older," Ella says as though she's a wise sage. "She always answered whatever I asked, no matter how silly."

"Silly how?"

"I don't know," Ella shrugged with an embarrassed chuckle. "I would ask her all kinds of stuff. Or I would say 'what's Dad doing right now?' like she would know."

"And what would she say?" he smiles, just as desperate to know about them, despite the sting to his heart. He wants to know everything they were doing while he was away.

"'Working.'"

He laughs and then quickly stops. Crying is too close on its heels.

"She was definitely right about that," he mutters, somewhat bitterly. "Did your mom ever have any um... boyfriends?"

Ella giggles into her hand, an unexpectedly jovial gesture that is signature Cynthia. His heart bursts into flames.

"What?" he grins, catching her contagious laughter.

"Mom's never had a boyfriend."

"Never, huh?" Ben grins even further with skepticism in his voice. He deduces that whoever she's been with since him hasn't been important enough to introduce to their daughter. A fact that both saddens him and gives him a special glee. He thinks it best to drop the subject with his daughter, however.

"We met a block from here, did you know that?"

"...Yeah, sort of."

"Sort of?"

"One time she pointed to it and said, 'I met your dad in that building right over there.'"

"But she didn't tell you who I was?" Ben smiled.

"No. I didn't like to push it after a while. I could tell it was hurting her feelings."

Ben fiddled with his ice cream in silence for a moment.

"Did she tell you why I wasn't around?"

"She just said that you didn't know about me, and that was to keep you safe. But at the right time, she would tell you and you would be here."

Keep him safe. For nearly an hour the anguish subsided and now it's back. A bittersweet mixture of sheer anger and gratitude.

He's grateful that Cynthia hasn't tarnished his image in her eyes. Now that they are talking, the anguish stings a little bit less.

"You know if I would've known about you, there would've been nothing that could keep me away. Your mom... did the smart thing, I guess. I'm glad she kept you safe. But I hate that I missed so much."

Ella frowned, reddening with emotion.

"Mom says there's still a lot to go," she said in a rasp.

"There is," he smiled. "She's very smart. We used to talk like this all the time. Just like you and me are talking now."

"Did you miss my mom?"

"All the time."

"Did you love my mom?"

"I did. I still do."

"Like... in that way?"

He huffs a laugh, his heart feeling so full at this little girl he's barely known 24 hours.

"Like, *in that way*, yes. I asked her to marry me. Did she tell you?"

Ella beams at first, and then her smile dissolves into tears. Ben's reaction mirrors hers as emotion is now choking him again as well.

"It's been an emotional two days, huh?" he manages to say.

She nods, wiping her blotchy face with a napkin.

"I hate crying."

"Like your mom," he chuckles. She nods, wiping her eyes with her arm.

"Just seems… too good to be true, I guess," she sniffs.

"It's not. Trust me. I hate that things happened the way that they have. I feel terrible that I just found out about you, meanwhile this entire time you've been waiting…"

Emotion begins waylaying him again. She handed him a napkin.

"Oh my *God*," he groans, feeling like a surfer getting pummeled by wave after wave. Finally, he feels composed enough to continue.

"Anyway, I don't wanna make it seem like I'm rushing in here to save the day or anything. I just got here, and I'm gonna make a lot of mistakes. Last time I talked to your mom I was… angry. When she told me about you. It felt like I was going to be mad at her for a lot longer, but. Honestly, now that you guys are back in my life, it's like I can't wait to see her again. But then again, I never could. She's the only woman I've ever loved. She never gave me an answer. About the whole 'marrying me' thing. I think she's gonna say no, but I gotta try."

Ella just listens to his speech with puffy eyes. "She won't say 'no.'"

"You don't think so?" he grins.

She shakes her head.

"She talks to you about this stuff?"

"No. But she doesn't have to. I know she still loves you."

"How do you know that?"

Ella quickly shrugs, chewing a piece of cookie dough out of her ice cream. "It's pretty obvious, Dad."

Ben chuckles. "You are one smart cookie, you know that?"

"She kept all your old messages."

"All my old messages?" Ben replies, a bit baffled. Ella nods.

"She got mad at me once," Ella relays between a lengthy bite. "For breaking the old phone with all your messages on it."

Ben stiffens. The days after she was gone, Ben called and called her old phone number in a stupor, until one day it'd disconnected and then become someone else's phone number. He sits stoically as the information washes over him.

"How long ago was that?"

"I was little. Really little. I just remember seeing it at the bottom of the toilet. I don't remember putting it in there or how I even got a hold of it. I just remember her yelling and scaring me. It's the only time she's ever yelled."

"She told you that was the reason? That my messages were on it?"

Ella nods. "Later, she did. When I asked her about it a couple years back. I was really mad at myself for that. I could've at least heard your voice."

"*Fuck*," Ben interjects with a sigh as he shakes his head. "Sorry," he says, coming back to his senses. He's quiet a little longer, obviously thinking, before he leans forward on his elbows, covering his face with both hands as if weary.

"*Fuuuuuuuck!*" he says again in a muffled groan, rubbing his hands over his face. "Sorry."

"People are looking at us."

"I'm sorry," he leans back in his chair, picking up his sundae. He shakes his head as he resumes eating.

"I didn't mean to make you upset."

"No, I know. It's okay. I'm glad you told me. It makes me really happy. More than happy, really, but it's just... that was a long time ago. Love can be kinda weird sometimes, Ella. Just because she kept those doesn't mean that still wants to be with me now. I really really messed up, Ell," he says, trying out her nickname, "and then when she told me about you, I just... freaked out. Just like she obviously predicted I would."

"But you still love her right? In that way?"

"With all my heart."

"Then she won't say no."

Ben sighed, "I trust your judgement, Ella."

"Anyway, I'll make sure she says 'yes,'" Ella responds, mimicking her Dad.

Ben puts his fist out for her to bump. She laughs and puts her fist out to meet his. He gives his double mocha fudge with sprinkles a few stabs with his spoon before he launches into his next question. "Ella, did you ever... meet... your grandfather?"

"Pop-pop?"

Ben stops, his spoonful of ice cream mid-way to his face.

"Kinda tall, white guy, curly hair, balding a little? Really rich?" she continues.

"How'd you know he's really rich?"

"I sorta guessed. He always has someone driving him. Gives me really weird, expensive gifts."

"How many times have you met him?"

"Not that many times."

"Did you know he's my dad?"

"Not 'til mom told me. Last night. She just said he was a friend of the family, and helped her with the business. I guess I understand why she lied to me, but I was mad. I can't believe I didn't guess."

"Well, he's really sick. He has Alzheimer's, do you know what that is?"

She nods.

"It might be a little scary, but I think he'd like to see you. But he might not recognize you. He's probably gonna… pass away. Soon. But you'll get to meet your Aunt Valerie. And maybe even your Uncle Grant. Would you like that?"

Ella quietly considers the proposition with a mouthful of ice cream.

"Can Mom come?"

Ben sighs, his mouth drawn down at the corners.

"I don't know if she would want to, but… I think I would want her to."

* * *

The following Saturday is easily the most bizarre day of Ben's life.

He finds himself in one of the brightest, sunniest hospital rooms ever, as if their expensive, researched decor could possibly fend off the air of death. His father is some frail thing he can hardly believe, sleeping and secured to a bed that looks more like a Star Trek prop. He's hooked up to machines since his brain is now too feeble to send messages for basic function.

In the room with him is his sister Val, his brother Grant, and

Cynthia. His daughter Ella has taken on the saintly duty of sitting with his mother, her grandmother, outside the room. Grant requested the two not be in the same room together as part of his agreement to fly in this weekend.

Grant has unexpectedly splayed himself over their father's frame in bed, inconsolable. It seems everyone has underestimated the gravity of this great loss, a giant redwood struck down in a sudden storm. Valerie is weeping into a tissue and Cynthia is sitting in the corner, her quiet energy somber and respectful. Ben looks over at her and she is simply looking out the window. She's been through this twice before, he realizes, and it is in circumstances like this he senses her great strength.

Their father suddenly wakes up and the atmosphere turns bizarre and wiry.

"Dad."

Solomon looks around a little, an oxygen mask on his face. His energy turns a little frantic and he's somehow able to move the bed, sensing he's restrained.

"Get Ella in here now," Val orders. There's a chance he's lucid and not just disoriented. Solomon looks back at them wordlessly and a little fearful.

"Dad, it's me. Grant," he sniffs, moving from his place on the bed. Sol looks at Grant when he says the name.

Sol doesn't believe the man, but he says Grant's name again, and then smiles a smile so recognizable that it brings tears to Sol's eyes, and he has to concede the man is telling the truth.

Instantly Ben understands what Val was trying to tell him, about wanting every moment she could get. The look in their father's face heals just about all of Grant's wounds on the spot.

"Daddy."

Solomon turns to Val, her voice and face clearly familiar to

228

him.

"Daddy, this is it," she says somberly, bravely. They've had this conversation before. He nods, shedding more tears, tears of relief.

"Dad," Ben barely eeks out. Solomon turns steely blue eyes to his son, whom he recognizes on sight. They've worked together every day for fifty years. Though he himself is only 30.

Solomon puts out a hand for his son to shake and Ben instantly takes it. Solomon won't let go, and he won't take his eyes off his son. Ben slowly dissolves into tears as his father's grip grows more and more firm, as firm as he can manage.

"Ella's here, Dad," Val says urgently, conscious of the clos- ing window. Solomon is still looking at Ben as if frightened, embarrassed. He remembers what he's done. Acutely.

"It's okay, Dad," Ben finds himself instantly forgiving with- out hesitation. "It's okay," he keeps saying, his father's unflinching stare begging for absolution.

Gingerly, Ella makes her way beside her dad, and everyone can see the smile on his face underneath the oxygen mask. He seems surprised, as though he were expecting to see a baby.

"Hi, Grandpa," Ella says in an emotional rasp, her face beet red, the tears flowing. A pair of tears fall down his own face at the sound of his proper title, once forbidden.

"Cynthia's here too," Ben volunteers. He waves her over hastily, trying to take advantage of their good fortune. Cynthia's holding her own balled up tissue when she makes her way over next to Ben and Ella.

"Wah say, boss man," Cynthia says as if it's an ordinary day and theirs is an ordinary relationship. She takes his open hand.

Instantly Solomon removes his hand from hers and reaches out towards Ben, summoning his. Ben takes his father's hand accordingly and Solomon pins it to the bed, grabbing Cynthia's hand again and putting it on top of Ben's. He puts his own liver-spotted hand on top them both, as if to keep them from separating. Ben looks over at her with an emotional smile as Cynthia nods wordlessly, crying.

"Mom," Val weeps, with a pleading look.

After a few seconds of hesitation, Molly Dvorak gets up from her chair and saunters over to her ex-husband, eyeing her newfound granddaughter for strength, the one he'd kept from them all. She gives Ella a kiss on the forehead before making her way to Sol's side.

The look they exchange is not one of love, but is still one of intense knowledge, and with it, understanding. Solomon doesn't recognize the woman but he recognizes the eyes. If Molly looks this old, then he must be very old indeed.

"You can rest now, Sol. Go on," Molly assures him, her double meaning not lost on anyone in the room.

Solomon reaches out for her hand and places it on his head, an ancient nighttime ritual of theirs. Molly blinks back tears as she loops her fingers around the thinning comb of curls on the top of his head. Solomon drifts peacefully to sleep amid a chorus of sniffs and sobs, looking like he's getting the best sleep of his life.

17

Present Day

"Thanks. For agreeing to come," Ben begins, looking and sounding exhausted as everyone slowly recovers from their poignant goodbyes. Ben approaches Cynthia in the corner of the room near the picture windows overlooking the skyline. Cynthia gathers her things as she speaks.

"Thanks for letting me be here," Cynthia says in an almost whisper. "I know I'm probably the last person you want to see right now. Ella wanted me here."

"Cynthia."

"What?"

"You're crazy if you think I'm still angry with you. Especially after today. Life's too short."

"...Even if I told you that he came to see Ella when she was a *baby* baby? Often?"

"It's in the past now."

"But I'm left holding his secrets."

"Don't. I'm telling you, I'm not angry. I don't understand why he did what he did. But I'm glad, somehow. The fact that he went to see Ella is completely mindblowing to me. I never knew he could be like that. Never in my wildest imagination would I ever come up with my father, closely guarding the secret knowledge that he was regularly hanging out with a baby. But I'm glad. I'm glad Ella got to see a different side to him. And you. Grant, Val, and I... maybe we were just too close to it. To see him another way. I'm glad he got to be this other person that he apparently wanted to be. Even if it wasn't with us."

"He told me to call him Sol, but I never could, not to his face," Cynthia whispered, looking over at the frail, sleeping man once her tyrant. "It started out as an intimidation tactic, I think. But then I got the feeling that he liked being around us. Val told me about the outbursts. Him saying Ella's name? Jesus. For some reason, I feel sorry for him, knowing he was that haunted."

"He isn't the only one," Ben shakes his head, "I thought just because I hated him and let him know it, that I was standing up to him. But he knew how much I needed his approval. All the way until he was no longer able to give it. I could've done more. I didn't."

"I could've done the hard thing too," Cynthia replies, "and I didn't. The truth is, I was probably more scared that you would try to make it all work. Figure out a way, like you always wanted. To have your fiancée of the day, have Ella, have the company, hell maybe me too, why not..." Cynthia looks down, shaking her head. "I couldn't bear that. Watching you move on. Having to share you. Forever. It was selfish."

"I wasn't moving on, I was... trying to find a woman who could keep me distracted long enough."

"Long enough for what?"

"Long enough to... I don't know. Forget you for a second. I just wanted to detach. I didn't want to find someone else so special that it would hurt so much to lose them."

"It doesn't work. Trust me," Cynthia whispers, unconsciously fiddling with the lapel of his jacket. She looks down, feeling remorseful.

Ben gives her a closed-mouth sigh of sadness, his fingers moving a piece of hair behind her ear. He holds her face in his hand.

"You walked in here today, with our daughter, and it made me feel invincible. It's like you're in color. And the rest of the world is black and white."

"Benji..."

"You're the love of my life, Cynth."

"You're mine," she reveals, hesitating only slightly as she focuses on both his eyes, his mouth, and back to his eyes again. She smiles, giving a little laugh.

"What?"

"I think this might be the first time we've been able to, you know, really love each other. Fully. No lies. Or secrets."

"I think you're right. Feels good."

"Some timing."

"Better now than never. I'm still waiting on that answer, by the way."

Cynthia grins.

"Kind of not the time or place for that, Ben."

"Cynth, you just got the old man's blessing. What better time is there?"

Ella picks the moment to saunter over to the whispering couple. Cynthia smoothes her hair with a hand, her way of asking if she's okay. But Ella is just looking at her father with a smirk. He sends one back and eyes Cynthia as she snickers.

"Ready, Ell?"

"Yeah. Dad, you coming?"

"Right behind you, just gotta finish up here. You did great, Ell, I'm proud of you. Thanks for coming."

"I brought Mom."

"I can see that. Thanks, kid. I owe you one."

"Ice cream?"

"It's a date."

"Oh yeah. I heard aaalll about your little after school special, Benji. And I do mean all of it," said Cynthia.

"Benjamin, honey, you're being rude."

Ben's mother sounds off from the side of his father's bed, monotonously beeping.

"Ma, Cynthia's gotta go."

"Cynthia, darling, Benjamin says you've got a waiting list a mile long."

"It's true, Molly, I do."

"You're such a doll, look at you. I told Benjamin he's gotta dump the model. We have to do lunch soon, we need to talk about my prospects."

"Prospects, Ma?"

"Benjamin, I need to be closer to Ella, and to do that you have to move me back to Jersey."

"Uh... we'll talk about it," Ben says as though fighting off a migraine. But Cynthia is secretly excited at the prospect of having family around again, the more hovering the better.

Cynthia makes her way over to Val who is sitting in a chair, looking far off. She kneels down in front of her demurely in her brown skirt, bright red pumps on her feet. Ben can't decipher what she says to her, but it seems to have no effect as Val continues to look away, dazed. Cynthia rights herself and returns to Ben's side.

"I'm taking the rest of the day off," Cynthia lowered her voice.

"You can have my answer tonight."

She means it to be respectful, but Ben doesn't take it there. He takes it somewhere else. The flirt in her eyes tells him that she knows what he's thinking and that she doesn't mind.

"I'm going to kiss you later. A lot," Ben gives her the PG version of his thoughts, mindful of the 9-year-old. Cynthia raises an eyebrow as she grins, already impressed at the sharpness of his fatherly instincts.

Cynthia takes Ella home with Ben ready to follow behind. Standing lonely in the hallway is Grant, having switched places now that his mother is inside. So smooth was his exit that Cynthia doesn't question it.

"It was good seeing you again, Grant."

"You too, Cynthia."

"Remind me when the two of you met?" Ben cocks his head.

"He came to the Dvorak building. During Thanksgiving."

"You weren't there," Grant fills in, cryptically.

"Grant here convinced me that the proper course of action was to break up with you. And that you would be upset for a while, but you would get over it. This was before I got fired, obviously."

Ben stands there wordless through this briefing. Cynthia puts a loving hand on his arm on the way out while Ben just stands there eyeing his brother in disbelief. The golden boy. He just got here and had no idea what was going on, and yet is somehow pivotal in his own life story.

"Congratulations, little brother. That's a real trophy wife you got there."

"Thanks. She hasn't said yes, yet."

"Clearly, she has. You always outdid me in the ladies department."

"Debateable. But you should try being a cripple."

235

"I'm done with all that, you know that, Ben."

"The vow of celibacy, I forgot. Good luck with that. Hey, how'd that vow of silence go?"

"So glib. I actually completed ten months of it. Ten."

"I— okay, Grant. Good job. Really. That might be the longest you've stuck to anything."

"Remember when Dad sent us to that prep school for boys?"

"How could I forget?"

"You'd just had your fifth surgery, just starting to walk on your own for the first time, which was the one dream in the world you allowed yourself to have... and he sent us to this shark pit... the moment you were physically able to go. There wasn't any pity for a kid like you in a place like that. Privilege either. It was lord of the fucking flies in there. I kept calling Mom and crying, begging her to get Dad to let us come home. I was confused, more than anything. I thought I'd done something to land myself in there."

"What's the point, Grant?"

"There is none. I was just thinking, I learned a lot from that. I learned how to be. Love, trust, loyalty, all of it's earned. And now I'm unlearning it."

"Me too," Ben mused, thinking of his dying father in the room behind them, Cynthia ahead of him. "I'm going back in there, you coming or what?"

"You know the rules."

Ben scoffs. "You were just in there with her."

"Val called her in, I can't help that."

"On a day like this? Grant? Isn't there something in your monk training about this?"

Suddenly, just as they're talking, the sound of nurses rushing up the stairs intensifies. They make their way to the end of the hall, where Ben and Grant eventually realize the nurses are headed for their father's room.

Grant immediately rushes in while Ben lets the cavalry pass and comes in slowly behind them, the horrid sound of the flatline taking command of the room.

Val has shielded her entire body from the scene by way of Grant's tall, overpowering frame. He too has elected to look away.

Their mother looks on in a rare bout of sincerity and strength, shedding no tears and mesmerized by the sight: her strong, intimidating groom who refused to smile on their wedding day, slipping away with a haunted expression.

"Mr. Dvorak, you're the only one authorized to allow us to resuscitate."

Ben stops looking at his father long enough to realize they're talking to him.

"Me?"

"Yes, sir."

Was that the old man's decision or Val's? He scans his faint memories of the last few weeks of meetings, but all he can see is Cynthia's check to his father. And her face.

Ben looks around at the room at his family for guidance. Val is buried in Grant's chest and done making decisions. Grant looks his crippled younger brother in the eye, assuring him that what he's thinking is the right decision. His mother just looks at him adoringly as she usually does, as if she still can't get over the fact that he's dressed himself.

"Mr. Dvorak?"

"No," Ben replies, a single tear slipping down his cheek undetected, "no, just... let him go. Do not resuscitate."

Once the machine is turned off, the distress begins to lift. His mother's voice is instantly blanketing the silence with phone calls and funeral arrangements, and he's never been so grateful for her to be the way she is.

Ben takes a moment of silence for the brutal way life is now steamrolling over his father's existence, making way for the next crop of souls busting through and needing out. He straightens his collar and clears his throat.

"If you all have this under control, I'm leaving."

"Already?"

"Yeah, Ma."

"Dinner later? I'm catching a plane tonight," Grant offers.

"Sounds good."

"I'll text you," Val says. "You going back to the office?"

"No," Ben nearly laughs in Val's face. He should probably tell someone soon that he has no intention of being the CEO of this company. That is now his, apparently.

"Then... where are you going?"

Ben smiles, finishing up a text reply to Ella, who has given up her and her mother's location.

"Home," Ben simply replies.

Epilogue

"A spa day, huh?"

"Yeah, just her and the girls. Cynth, my mom, Ell, Val..."

Ben planted his shovel upright in the dirt and leaned on it, facing the sun until he had to yield and shield his vision. Sweat trickled down his forehead and threatened to get into his eyes.

"So's that like a... all day thing, or..."

"All weekend. They just got back last night."

"All weekend? Wow. Must've been nice having the man cave to yourselves, huh boss?"

Ben could only nod listlessly. His breath seemed endlessly lost and his lungs ached in protest. He wiped his forehead and immediately lamented, forgetting for a split second that he was covered in dirt. He felt the grit of mud now caking in the wrinkles of his brow. A few of the guys on the crew laughed, including their manager, Vito.

"Maybe you should call it a day, boss."

"I'm not the boss," Ben panted.

"Sure boss," Vito replied.

"But I am gonna take you up on that, Vito."

"You did good, boss," he said.

"Really?"

Vito gave him an incriminating look of "please don't ask me to lie." He broke into a smile he couldn't hold back, and finally a laugh.

Ben smiled and shook his head, trying not to feel defeated.

"Hey. Thank God you're good with numbers, huh, boss?"

"Thank God, indeed."

"We got this. You just keep writin' those checks, boss!" another on the crew piped up.

"I will. Anybody else need water?"

"Nah, we're good," Vito shouted among the snickering as Ben made it back to his car. He was filthy and he didn't care. He turned the key and didn't even flinch when hot summer air blew full force out of the vents. Finally, he'd regained enough strength to start the car and head home.

* * *

"Oh Lord, Vito," Cynthia moaned, talking to Vito on her way home from work. Wally, who was almost four, was strapped in the backseat asleep.

"We didn't work him too bad, boss."

"Why did you even let him talk you into working with the crew in the first place?"

"You try talking him out of it. Figured if he got a good enough taste he'd stop suggesting."

"How's that plan workin' out so far?"

"We had to dig trenches today, and I didn't let him use the jackhammer. That should keep him away for at least a year or two."

When Cynthia got to the large house on Moss Lane, she saw Ben's car covered in dirt and parked neatly under the carport where she pulled up next to it. Gingerly, she removed Wally from his seat, but it was no use. As soon as the car stopped, he was awake for good.

She opened the back door off the kitchen where she was instantly greeted by a pile of dirt-caked pants and a shirt vaguely headed in the direction of the laundry room. She chuckled. *Poor thing*, she thought.

She got to the living room where Ella was sprawled out on the couch, her schoolwork scattered around her and the tv on, watching MeTV videos.

"Where's Grandma?"

"Home."

"Can you go over there and tell her Wally's up from his nap?"

"I can text her."

"Or you can get your young, spry little bottom up off the couch and walk across the street, like I asked you."

"I'm sort of waist deep in algebra right now."

Cynthia sighs a rare sigh of resignation.

"Fine. Text her right now, please. Where's your dad?"

"Upstairs, I think."

"You think?"

"Hasn't been downstairs since I got home from school."

"Did you... check on him?"

"...No?" Ella answered as though it were a trick question.

Cynthia sighed and put down a squirming Wally who instantly climbed into his sister's lap.

"You know you can have friends over if you want, Ell. Just let us know."

"I know."

"If there was something going on at school, you'd tell me. Right?"

"...Probably."

Good enough, Cynthia thought with a sigh as she headed upstairs.

241

She gingerly opened the door to their bedroom, not quite sure what to expect. When she saw Ben sprawled out face down on the bed, his hair still slightly damp and a towel around his middle, she was overcome with a fit of giggles. She kicked her shoes off and laid across the head of the bed where there was ample room. When he still hadn't moved, she had to laugh some more.

"What did I say, Ben? I said, 'stop.. trying.. to go out there.. and kill yourself in the hot sun with those guys. Your family needs you.'"

"What kind of man... can't dig a ditch?"

"You have... so, many, other talents, Benji."

"It's not a 'talent' to dig ditches, Cynth. It's a necessity for survival."

"Okay, you have so many other... important traits to bring to the table that ensure our survival."

"Name one."

"I can name more than one, Benji. You broker deals. You find us properties. You spend all day at the zoning office without losing your mind."

"Does anyone's life depend on it? Will it keep you all from starving?"

"Yes, in a roundabout way. Those guys out in the hot sun all day are good at what they do, and we pay them well to do what they're good at, but you still get paid more."

"Because I'm married to their boss."

"No, because the talent you have is *rare.* Not every man can do what you do, and they would switch places with you in a heartbeat if they could."

"That's because I get to schtup you."

Cynthia laughed again at her pitiful husband. His hands were covered in cuts and forming callouses. She kissed his knuckles, the skin near his wedding band.

"So... Esmee finally picked a venue."

"That's great," Ben grunted as he rolled over onto his back.

Esmee Ngozi was engaged to her longtime manager Nigel Starr. They were madly in love and Esmee had been dragging her feet, deciding which venue she wanted to serve as the "vehicle for Cynthia Gordon's inspiration."

Cynthia wasn't particularly confident she could design for a wedding, but she'd dabbled in the planning of her own nuptials five years ago and was already starting to get inspired. Theirs was a stuffy, high-profile nightmare, and Esmee's would likely follow suit. The best parts of the wedding that the press ranted and raved about were all things that Cynthia had personally handled, including her dress which was the first and last one she ever had to try on. Her very expensive Parisian wedding planner never saw fit to set the record straight, which chaps Cynthia's professional ass to this day. She was gonna make sure her name was allll over this one.

There was no bad blood between Cynthia and Esmee, however, because they were now best friends. Sisters really. Breaking up with Ben was rough for Esmee, but not as rough as she would've liked. She had to concede Ben wasn't the one. But once he and Cynthia got together, it was as though their relationships snapped in proper alignment like a spine. Esmee often joked that gaining Cynthia Gordon as a sister was worth two Benjamin Dvoraks.

"It's going to be in Essex, so it looks like I'll be able to make the pilgrimage."

"I'm happy for you, hon. *And* you'll be getting paid for it."

"...About that."

"Cynthia Dvorak, please tell me you charged that *very* wealthy woman *actual* money to do this."

"...I gave her a very deep discount."

"Cynthia..."

"It's very deep. I'm not gonna lie."

"I knew you should've let me talk to her. Lemme guess, she wants you to be *in* the wedding as well?"

Cynthia sighed.

"Okay fine, I'll re-negotiate."

"Thank you."

"...Actually, can you do it?"

"I will gladly do it."

"God, I love having you around."

"I love being around."

"She told me the strangest story. About you."

Ben sighed and rolled his eyes. "If it's about sex, I don't want to hear it."

Cynthia giggled a giggle of guilt.

"*She* said..." Cynthia continued anyway, "that on the first night you introduced us, that you were so... *hot and bothered*," Cynthia attempted Esmee's English accent, "that you basically had sex in the cab on the way home."

"Honestly, the two of you are way too close."

"Benji, how could you have sex in a cab with her, but not with me?"

"We didn't have *sex* in a cab, Cynth, just... subject change."

"Fine. Would you please... stop... trying to do manual labor?"

"The roofers said the bricklayers have it easy compared to them."

"Ben, *don't*."

"I won't. Anyway, right now, I can't. The thought of it is painful."

"I don't even know where all this is coming from. You said you didn't mind slumming it as a millionaire. All you wanted to do is work honestly for once, you said. That's what you're doing."

Ben sighed. "I don't know, it's just... Val was telling me about this deal they just closed."

Val was announced as the successor and had taken over Ben's position at the Dvorak Group when their father died six years ago. Grant tried to jockey for the position, but the board wasn't going for that. When Val and Ben used their seats to go against him, he had a new excuse to hold a grudge against the family and went back to being a monk.

Val didn't have a finance background. But she knew a thing or two about politics. Her first order of business was to fire Doug. She let Ben sit in on that little meeting.

"Ben, if you wanted to go back, you know all you would have to do is say the word."

"I thought you needed me here?"

"I do. But I need you to be content, more than I need you here."

"I was never content there. That place chews you up."

"Not Val, she's crushing it. She's never been happier."

"She's a natural. Dad saw it. But look at her marriage, it's ripped to shreds."

"Pretty sure Sol's death had more to do with that. And by 'Sol's death' I mean her husband's infidelity."

"It's been six years and it's still weird not having him around. Or having this company that was such a big part of my identity. The big desk."

"Admit that you feel weird working for me. You won't hurt my feelings."

245

"I love that you're the boss of me and you know that."

"Then what's the deal?"

"I guess I'm just in a hurry to see that my life makes a difference. On its own."

"Benji..." Cynthia sighed.

"Don't."

"Don't what?"

"Don't try to comfort me, I know I'm insane."

"You're not. Believe it or not, I understand. And I know I could say a bunch of things to try and convince you that Wally is the obvious proof that your life matters, or that having you in our lives makes us feel whole and healthy in a way that we didn't expect, but you'd just dismiss it. Because you'll always feel like the luckier one. I'm telling you, I get it."

"You do understand."

"One day, you'll look around and see it for yourself."

"You really wanna have sex in a cab?"

Cynthia gave him a slight smile, her light eyes sparkling as she reached across him, her arm making its way down his chest where his towel was still in place.

Just then, they heard the door creak. Ben groaned.

"I think we've got company," Cynthia smiled.

"Walter," Ben beckoned, knowing it was his son. Wally came running in prepared to jump on the bed.

"Careful, Wally, your daddy's hurting," Cynthia warned. He jumped on the bed anyway.

"Well daddy, I wanna play blocks," Wally astutely replied.

"We will. In a minute, buddy. Go set it up."

Wally decided to just stay put. Ben examined him in his heightened existential state, looking into Wally's bright blue-gray eyes. He shared the same creamy shade of his sister, a bit

246

richer than Ben's own. Wally examined him right back for a brief humbling moment before his stubby hand was splayed across his father's face, assuming this staring game needed some spice. Wally laughed. Ben smiled. And Cynthia looked on from her place on the bed, wondering how the hell could a person be this lucky.

I Love Reviews!

Yes, even the critical ones (sort of)! Did you like the book? Which part was your favorite? Was the sex too much? Not enough? Anything stand out to you that you've never read before, or haven't seen in awhile? Anything you could've done without, perhaps? Well I wanna know!!

Besides that, when it comes to choosing the next great read, reviews can make or break, whether you're an indie author like me, or one of the big fish in a New York Publisher's pond.

Believe it or not, you can help. A LOT.

And all it will cost you is about a dozen words or more.

If you enjoyed this book at all, and think others should too, please take five minutes to leave this book a review on the page of your respective ebook retailer. Thank you!

Have You Joined the Mailing List Yet?

If you like what you've read, I would like to keep in touch with you!

- Find out about new releases, limited time deals and bonus content!
- Get access to fan exclusives from the *Billionaire's Club* series!
- Get to know me and what I'm up to, and even work with me as part of my Advance Team!

Simply click on the link, and enter your email address to sign up:

https://www.subscribepage.com/CLDMLLanding

About the Author

C.L. Donley is a future New York Times and USA Today Best-selling Author of multicultural and interracial romance. Armed with a B.A. in English and M.A. in Writing, she is new to the romance game, having written her first novel, Amara's Calling, after discovering the romance genre in September 2017. Her writing style is sophisticated yet simple, unaplogetically escapist and character driven. She likes to write loveable, redeemable and believable characters and place them in equally loveable, romantic and relatable settings and scenarios— removed from reality just enough so that the reader can properly escape, and even revisit!

You can connect with me on:

🌐 https://cldonley.com

🐦 https://twitter.com/C_L_Donley

f https://facebook.com/amarascalling

🔗 https://bookbub.com/authors/c-l-donley

Subscribe to my newsletter:

✉ https://www.subscribepage.com/CLDMLLanding

Also by C. L. Donley

Love on a Lark

Lark Chambers is young, beautiful and brilliant, an interpreter fluent in seven languages. When a handsome stranger christens her first night in her favorite city of Florence with lovemaking, Lark finds herself confronting the turmoil behind her put- together exterior. And her latest assignment working for Dario DiRossi just might put her over the edge.

Leftovers With Benefits

C.L. Donley fan favorite! When Kenya's husband Cecil unexpectedly leaves her for a white woman, she finds solace with the most unlikely new ally: Kevin Hayes, the other woman's ex.

The Billionaire's Club Trilogy

Amara and Grayson: the hot, quirky couple that started it all. Mya and Dale: the controversial pairing that no one saw coming, especially the two of them. Kim and Bel: the undercover royals who fall in love at first sight.

Spend all day in la la land jet setting with this "plane Jane meets billionaire" trilogy about three couples that are as different as the individuals are from each other. Exotic locales, destination weddings, sex contracts, secret babies, and all the "happily ever afters" you could ever want!